DEATHLESS

by Graveyard Greg

Deathless

Copyright © Graveyard Greg
2010

Cover Artwork by Forgewielder
Interior Illustrations by Genesis and Sudonym

Published by Argyll Productions
Dallas, Texas
www.argyllproductions.com

ISBN 978-1-935599-62-3

Printed in the United States of America
First Edition Trade Paperback 2010

ACKNOWLEDGEMENTS

To Genesis and Sudonym, who took the time to grace their art for the book's interior!

To Forgewielder, who took the time to make the cover for Deathless.

To Anima and Ben Goodridge for their editing prowess.

I would also like to thank Cannon, Eric Easterly , Michael Knabusch, Brady Hagan, Srass, Tyco, Matthew Pursley, Taylor Fultz, Shane Patrick, Brent Dorsey, the Amazing Adrian, Zato Dragon, Serena El-Farra, Breve, Conner Coon, Rob Calhoun, John Yakimow, Ceithen, Brophey, Scott "Atpaw" Boyd, and Gaby Fullerton.

Thanks to Iron Spike and Kickstarter for making this book possible.

Finally, all my love to the very patient boyfriend of mine.

PROLOGUE

The sun's rays filtered through the canopy of trees, warming the snow leopard while he shoveled more dirt from the ground. The hole was shoulder deep now, but Mikhail hadn't found any sign of the chest. He pulled out the map from the inner pocket of his Thinsulate vest, his eyes darting back and forth from the tree, with its thick roots and wide trunk, to the map and its handwritten notes.

Even as sure as he was, could he have made a mistake? Might his search, which spanned several weeks--precious time he could have spent with his wife Victoria and little Ivan--be in vain? If so, then he had failed his family, and surely they would suffer even more for his foolish endeavor.

"*Nyet*," Mikhail mumbled as he folded up the map before returning it to his vest pocket. The thoughts stubbornly clung to him, trying to slow down his efforts. They tried to make him give up and go back to the motherland. Perhaps he should. He missed his wife and son. Maybe they could make do with their meager wages. Maybe they could--

The shovel clanked against something hard. A rock, perhaps? Or...

The dirt flew away from Mikhail in wide arcs, the shovel a blur of motion in his excitement. What he struck was no rock. He saw wood, then the glint of gold.

It was the chest, the reason he had spent weeks traveling and endured days of seasickness. All for this moment.

As Mikhail pulled the chest out of the earth, he was surprised by how new it looked. The gold plating lacked even a spot of tarnish. The iron lock was absent of rust. Even the dirt failed to cling to its surface. If he had not known of the chest's origins, he would have believed it had been buried a few hours ago.

He easily picked the lock, then drew his revolver. A quick flick of his wrist revealed the chambers were full of bullets. He snapped the cylinder shut before carefully lifting the lid open.

A white blur leaped out of the chest, followed by the deafening thunder of his shot. Damn, it was quick! Still, he scored a definite kill. He quickly took aim at the dead rabbit that bled into the ground. So far everything he read was true. So next would be--

There was a fierce flapping of wings as the duck miraculously emerged from the rabbit's muzzle. Mikhail ended its struggles with another shot from his pistol. Heart beating thunderously within his chest, he approached the fowl.

In front of the dead bird was an egg; its shell was a perfect white, like the snow that blanketed his homeland in winter. His ears swiveled around, and his eyes squinted as he made a quick circle around him. He was certain that he was being watched--the hackles on his neck were certainly raised enough to prove that--but after minutes of silence and seeing nothing but the trees and the dead rabbit and duck, he finally dismissed it as paranoia. The only living thing was himself.

Mikhail scooped up the loose dirt under the egg, placing his other paw on top of it as he cradled it against his chest. Everything he'd been told about this chest since childhood had been true. He had found the egg. He had found his family's future.

His life would not be the same again.

CHAPTER 1

"Hey dude! Look! I have a road on my arm!"

Ivan glanced up from his textbook to see his roommate, a white rabbit, flexing his arm. He had a new tattoo, a highway dyed around the fur of his biceps muscle. He was wearing nothing but a pair of boxers with hearts decorating the fabric. This was nothing new, but Ivan immediately pulled his attention back to the textbook.

"Ain't it sweet, Latté?"

Ivan grimaced, his round ears flattening against his skull as his fur started to floof. "Please, Brady," he growled, "do not call me by that nickname."

"Aw, come on, dude. Call me Hopper."

Brady...Hopper...claimed to hate his first name for the reason it made him feel like a grandfather. Ivan could not understand why. His own grandfather was loved. Didn't Hopper want to be loved?

"Hey Hopper!" A hyena, slightly larger than the rabbit, entered the bedroom. He was wearing blue bikini briefs and a green hat with the UNR logo. He held a beer can between thumb and forefinger as usual. "Did I just hear you say you got a road on your arm?"

Hopper nodded, turning to face the hyena as he flexed again. "Yeah, man! Check it! I have a road on my arm!"

"Fuckin' *sweet!*"

Ivan's thick, spotted gray tail swept across the floor as he started to finger the yin-yang pendant on his necklace. He never had this kind of habit until he came to America on his student visa, and the habit grew worse when he moved into the dorm.

"Hopper. Dude. You gonna go to the party this Saturday?" the hyena

3

asked after taking a long swallow of his beer.

"Heck yeah, Eric. It's gonna be awesome!"

"Gonna be a fuck-ton of bitches there."

"Aw, yeah. And a lot of hot guys."

Ivan stole a glance at the two, his eyes gravitated to Hopper's sculpted, muscular butt. He could make out half of the name dyed on the rabbit's fur: Larry? Labby? Before he could decipher it Hopper started to turn around, so he quickly looked away.

"Dude, were you looking at my ass?" Hopper asked.

"N-nyet. I vas going to ask if you and Eric vould please to leave bedroom." Ivan glanced up. Both Hopper and Eric were smiling toothy grins. His tail lashed even faster.

"Hopper, I think our snow leopard buddy needs to get some tail."

"Hell yeah! When's the last time you had a good lay, Latté?"

"Lay? Vhat is lay?" Ivan hated asking for definitions.

Hopper grinned. "Sex, man. When's the last time you had sex? Back in Russia?"

"I...I do not have sex. Too busy for studies and going to gym."

Hopper slapped a paw on Ivan's shoulder, squeezing it. "Dude, you can afford to skip a day. You're, like, solid muscle under all that fluff!"

"I...I just vant to continue my studies, please." Ivan lifted up his book, trying to read the same page for the fifth time.

"Dude! You know who would be perfect for a big guy like you?" Hopper didn't wait for an answer. "My cousin! He's big like you. He'd be just the guy!"

"Please do not be going through trouble--"

4

"It's no trouble, dude! Trust me!"

Bozhe moi, thought Ivan.

Hopper lived up to his name as he hopped in place on his long, wide paws. Ivan looked on nervously at his little bookshelf on the wall, certain that the rabbit's eagerness would cause the books to fall. "Dude, I'm totally going to call him right now before he goes to work!"

"Doesn't he work as a bouncer at a bar?" Eric leaned against the door frame, taking a long swallow of his beer.

"Yeah, I better hurry. The cell reception there's lousy as shit." Hopper ran out of the bedroom, and Ivan released a breath he hadn't realized he was holding all this time.

Eric smirked down at the snow leopard. "Dude, you are so wound up."

"Vound up?" Some American slang went over Ivan's head. This one left enough room for Eric to walk under.

"Yeah. You're tense. You worry too much."

"It is hard not to vorry."

Eric tittered rapid, high pitched laughter. It hurt Ivan's ears. "You have a killer accent, Latté."

"You have killer accent as well."

Eric tilted his head, looking blankly at Ivan. "Huh? I don't have an accent."

"To my ears, you have accent. All Americans have accent."

Eric's ears perked up, and his tongue almost lolled out of his muzzle as it split open into a grin. "Oh! I getcha now. Yeah, I guess I would have an accent to you."

"Yes. Now, if I could ask you to be leaving." He tapped the page he'd been trying to read. "I need to finish studying."

Eric looked at the book, and for a moment stood there silently as if he were trying to grasp the concept of studying. He finally blinked, and nodded. "Oh yeah, sure thing, big guy! No problem."

As Eric closed the door behind him, Ivan felt himself relax. He could finally finish his reading assignment for World History and--

The door flew open, slamming up against the wall as Hopper bounded in. Ivan held up the book in front of him as a shield. "*Dude!*"

"*Vhat?*"

Hopper flinched, ears folding back. "Dude, you don't gotta yell. You scared the shit outta me."

Scared *him?* Ivan's fur had fluffed out thanks to him! He'd need to find his brush and spend at least an hour combing himself down. "Vhat is it, Hopper? Please, I must finish reading assignment!"

"I just called my cousin, and he said he'd come over tomorrow before work to meet you."

"I do not vish to meet people." It was a lie. A bad one, and Hopper knew it.

"Dude, you were saying last week how you wanted to meet more people. Here's your chance."

"I do not know if I can be meeting your cousin."

"Listen, Latté, if you meet my cousin I'll buy you your lattés for a week."

Ivan perked his ears forward. "For a veek?"

Hopper nodded. "A whole, solid week."

"Starting tomorrow." Lattés were expensive. If he didn't have to buy his favorite coffee for a week, it might be worth meeting someone, even someone like Hopper's cousin.

"Deal!"

"So hey, you wanna go grab a latté right after I call my cousin?"

Ivan almost said yes, but the textbook in his hands reminded him of his obligation. "*Nyet.* I really must study."

"You sure, dude? You've been studying ever since you got home."

"I am certain. After studies, I must go to gym to exercise. Then come back to study more."

"Geez, dude, you study more than me and Eric both."

"I must keep good grades to keep student visa. If I do not, I vould have to go back home. To Russia."

Hopper's ears flicked a bit, then drooped down. "Oh yeah. I didn't think about that. It'd be, like, embarrassing to you, huh?"

"Poppa has worked all his life to make certain my momma, my brother and I vould be taken care of. I must honor his dedication."

"I guess I'll leave you alone, and get you a latté later if you need to pull an all-nighter. That okay with you?"

Ivan smiled. "That vould be acceptable. Thank you."

The soft click of the door closing shut brought a sigh of relief from Ivan. Now he could finally study without any interruption from his roommates.

But his thoughts were not so considerate. Now he imagined going home in failure. To face the disappointment of his family. A mother who worked just as hard as his father to keep the house together. A younger brother who looked up to him. Could he stand to return home in shame and disgrace?

No, he couldn't.

He closed the book, keeping a finger on the page he had continuously failed to study. The weight of familial obligation was heavy on his mind, and he could almost feel the weight on his shoulders. He shoved away those dark thoughts and left the bedroom to get to the phone in the living room. Ivan was going to get his wallet out for his international phone card, then wondered if it was too early to call his family. He was terrible at converting the time. Would they be sleeping?

As he padded into the living room, Hopper and Eric were bent over the aquarium near the kitchen. They looked as tense as he felt, and there was a faint scent of worry from Hopper.
"She doesn't look good, dude," Eric whispered.

"I think she's dying," Hopper said. Was there a hitch in his voice?

Ivan moved over to the two, looking over their shoulders to view Hopper's pet iguana in the aquarium. She was still as a pond, which was nothing new. She rarely moved unless it was time to eat or she wanted to move to a warmer spot. What differed this time was she was on her back, her eyes looking upwards at nothing. "Perhaps," he said quietly, "she is just sleeping."

Hopper shook his head, glancing up at Ivan. "She never sleeps with her eyes open."

Her scales were a light green, with the dewlap on her chin a darker coloration. Ivan wondered how she could rest on her back like that. Wouldn't her spines cause her discomfort?

"Dude, give her a nudge. Maybe she's sleeping."

Hopper shook his head. "I think she's dead, man." He looked up at Ivan. "Does she look dead to you, dude?"

Ivan blinked, glancing down at the iguana. Her eyes were black pools. Empty. Lifeless. "She is not breathing," he finally said. His mouth felt strangely dry.

Hopper flinched at the news. "D-damn," he said, biting down on the knuckle of his thumb.

"I guess we need a garbage bag," Eric said, taking a swallow of his beer.

Hopper turned on Eric. "*Dude!*" His eyes were open wide, a scowl on his face. Hands were balled up into tight, trembling fists. "Cannon is *not* going into the garbage!"

Ivan placed his hands on Hopper's shoulders, wedging himself between the two. "No fighting. You are both friends. You will be calming down now, Hopper."

Hopper pointed at Eric around Ivan's broad shoulders. "He wants me to get a garbage bag for Cannon!"

Ivan eyed Eric, who was shaking his head during Hopper's tempest. "No, dude. I wasn't suggesting throwing away your iguana. We just need to put her in something to take to the vet."

Hopper's eyes were angry, yet glassy, unspent tears pooling up around the corners. "The vet? She's dead. Why would I take her to the vet?"

"Because the vet can take care of the body, man."

Hopper suddenly tried to lunge past Ivan to grab Eric, but the snow leopard's grip was firm. All he managed to do was press up against Ivan. "I'm not letting some stranger bury Cannon!"

Eric took a step back, hands held up in front of him. The empty beer can bounced along the carpet. "Jesus, dude. Okay. Calm down, we'll bury

Cannon somewhere, but we should at least put her in the bag. Keep the smells out and stuff."

The explanation seemed to calm down Hopper. He lowered his arm and backed off of Ivan. "Yeah. I guess that'll work."

"I didn't mean to piss you off, Hopper."

"It's...all right. Cannon was with me for a long time. Ten years." His voice wavered. "Maybe...maybe she was just old."

Ivan released Hopper, hoping the rabbit would remain calm. "I am sorry for your loss."

"Thanks, Ivan. I'm gonna...I'm gonna go lay down after I put Cannon in..." He sank to his knees, his outstretched fingers brushing the glass of the aquarium. "I need to be alone here, guys. I don't know if I'm gonna cry, but I might. I don't want you guys to see that."

Eric nodded. "Okay." He disappeared into his bedroom, closing the door.

Ivan took the cordless phone with him, turning it on as he entered his room.

Nothing happened.

He tried again. The phone was dead. He quietly returned to the living room and saw Hopper with his head against the aquarium glass. Either he didn't notice Ivan, or was ignoring him. The snow leopard placed the phone on the charger and returned to his bedroom. He would call his family tomorrow.

Ivan put on a tank top, grabbed the gym bag next to his bed, and saw Hopper was no longer in the living room. The front door was ajar. Hopper forgot to shut it behind him again, but it was understandable. He still hoped Hopper hadn't left in his boxers.

Ivan looked at the dead iguana staring at the ceiling. A strange chill started to fill his body, but he shrugged it off.

**

He was relieved to be away from the apartment.

The nighttime sky had almost overwhelmed the last vestiges of the day, but the red skies clung to the Sierras, illuminating Ivan's walk to the gym. It was a short walk, even shorter when he jogged, and it gave him time to decompress his tired, over-studied mind.

His tail was now elevated and swaying to and fro as he approached the gym, his ears perked forward. He found it easier to breathe now that he was out of the stressful situation inside the apartment. His father would approve of a decision to take a break from studies--working hard was a good thing, but overworking one's self was not.

"One must remember to feed the inner child, or else suffer its tantrums," the elder Andreev would frequently say.

Even though he was a history professor at the Saint Petersburg University, his father would take time for his hobbies. There was a shelf filled with his collection of dice. Six siders, four siders--even a seven sider, which always fascinated Ivan when he was a child.

"God does not play dice with the universe," his father once said, "but I do."

Ivan would call his family as soon as he returned to the apartment. The phone would be fully charged, and he would be able to catch up on the family's events. Granted, he could email them, but that was so impersonal. There was nothing better than to hear the gravelly voice of his father, the doting tone of his mother's, and even the annoying voice of his little brother, whose body was quickly filling out into the shape of manhood.

A low, droning buzz soon distracted him from his thoughts, and a small, black-banded bumblebee, its legs coated with pollen, flew around his head. His ears twitched, and he fought to keep from panicking. Bumblebees could sting multiple times, and he was deathly afraid of being stung. He was mildly allergic to them, and while his thick coat might protect him, it could always sting him in the less protected areas like his nose. So being stung was something he wanted to avoid at any cost.

Ivan wasn't even sure the bee was still buzzing around him. He did not want to take the chance of being stung, so he broke out into a run, leaping over the small ditch that separated the apartment complex from the shopping center that had recently been built. From there, the gym was across the street, and he slowed down when he reached the gym's parking lot. He leaned forward, hands on his knees as he caught his breath.

Then he heard the buzzing growing louder again. Looking up in alarm, he saw the fuzzy gold and black insect flying towards him. He rushed inside, then felt a sharp pain on his tail. At first he thought he was stung, but then saw his tail had gotten caught by the closing door. He pulled in his tail, the blush burning his ears.

Genesis '09

Something moved out of the corner of his vision. The bee crawled up the glass, as if saying *I'll be waiting for you.*

He swore it *winked* at him.

There was a trio with their backs to the door, wolves from the brief glance Ivan gave them. His progress temporarily blocked, Ivan watched the bee crawl up the door, its yellow body stood out against the darkening night sky. He forced himself to take slower breaths and smoothed down the fluffed out tailtip, but what if someone came in from the outside? What if there was a crack in the door? What if this insect discovered the crack, and continued its relentless pursuit of the snow leopard?

What if. What if. Ivan chuckled at his foolish fears, but then felt a bit of fright as the bee turned around 180 degrees and moved downward towards him. It paused once it reached his eye level, and stared at him. He knew it was staring at him, though with its multifaceted eyes there was no real way he could prove his tiny six-legged stalker was indeed focused on him.

It then spread its wings, and took flight into the night. Ivan sighed with relief, shoulders slumping from the ease of tension.

The tension returned when the bee suddenly thudded against the glass; Ivan immediately stepped back, startled. What was wrong with this bumblebee? Had Ivan unconsciously committed some terrible wrong against it or its hive queen? "*Bozhe moi!*" he muttered as he struggled to tear his eyes away from the bee. Certainly it would leave if he moved further into the gym. The trio was no longer in sight, so he quickly made his way inside.

Standing behind the reception desk was a large white rabbit in a black tank top and pants. Broad shouldered, ears erect, and grinning warmly at him. "That bee has it in for you, huh?"

Ivan set his gym bag down at his feet, nodding. Something about the rabbit was familiar, but he couldn't place it. He had never met him before. "I am afraid of bee stinging." Ivan didn't know why he was explaining this, but he felt it was proper.

"Allergic?" the rabbit asked as he handed Ivan the sign-in sheet.

Ivan nodded as he put down his name and ID number. "It is not pleasant, being stung. Hurts to swallow after for some time. At vorst, I go to hospital." Why was he being so talkative? Perhaps it was the warmth the rabbit radiated from the smile. It was a good smile.

"Don't worry..." The rabbit's voice trailed off briefly as he glanced at the sign-in sheet. "...Ivan, is it? I'll swat any bee that comes near you."

Ivan chuckled sheepishly. "*Spasiba.*"

The tall rabbit quirked an eyebrow as his grin faded. "What?"

"Oh. I am sorry. It means thank you."

"Huh. So you're from another country?"

Ivan nodded. "*Da*. Am Russian."

The grin returned. "Now you're just showing off."

Ivan's eyes grew wide, and he shook his head quickly. "*N-nyet*! I did not mean to offend!"

"Hey, relax. I was just kidding." The rabbit chuckled weakly, scratching his head. "Guess I look too serious." He then extended a hand. "Name's Angus, but my friends call me Tank."

Ivan took the hand. The rabbit's grip was firm; Ivan also noticed he had to look up at Tank, and he was seven feet tall! "Pleasure to meet you, Tank."

"Pleasure's all mine, Ivan."

As Ivan went to the locker room to change, he suddenly thought of haystacks and how Tank was as big as one. An odd thought, but one to make him chuckle.

He then sobered up as his mental gears shifted to Hopper. Where did he go? Ivan hoped his roommate would not do anything foolish like suicide. That would be quite the extreme reaction over the death of a pet, no matter how loved it was. No, Ivan would not--could not--believe Hopper would ever get that distraught. In many ways, the rabbit reminded him of the surfer people in the movies. They lived life without any worries, and so did Hopper.

And yet...was that not false? Hopper certainly *did* have worries. The death of his iguana was proof of that. It was the first time he'd seen Hopper emotionally distraught. The iguana was like family to him.

Family. He was reminded of how far apart he was from his own. They were on the other side of the globe. Did they miss him as much as he missed them? Most likely, as they were a close-knit unit. It was difficult for them to decide that Ivan should go to America to study, and he almost refused to go.

It was ultimately his father who gave him the motivation to come overseas.

"It will be good life experience, to go to the land of opportunity," his father said. "It is a land of freedom. Something Russia is still trying to become."

So Ivan gave in to his father's request. He tried his best to embrace the culture with some success, but his home, his heart, would belong to his family. He would call them as soon as he returned to the apartment. It would chase away the growing homesickness in his heart.

The workout went without difficulty, although Ivan exercised alone. No one offered to help spot him, so he usually went to the machines for the heavier routines. But whenever possible, he used the free weights. They were far more challenging to use, since he was forced to use the proper form on his own rather than be assisted by mechanical devices.

His thoughts moved to the old barn at home. Inside was a workout bench with several weights. His father owned that bench, and started training him when he was old enough to understand the responsibility and dedication required to get in shape. Then his younger brother was introduced to their workout routines, and soon all three were determined to get stronger and healthier.

Now he was alone. His father and younger brother most likely worked even harder in his absence. But they only needed to replace him. He had to replace both.

He would talk to his family soon, and the conversation in their native tongue would lift his spirits, and perhaps their own.

He hoped his run home would be free from stalker bees.

The locker room was empty, which was fine by Ivan. He preferred privacy for his post-workout shower, but it was usually too crowded for his comfort levels. He quickly undressed and entered the stall. The water was ice cold against his fur, and he kept it that way. The temperature reminded him of the times he and his father would go swimming in the dead of winter. It was something only he and his father were willing to do--his mother and younger brother didn't care for that particular winter activity.

He remembered the odd looks Hopper and Eric gave him when he asked where the apartment pool was located. It was January, and the ground had been colored white with a recent snowfall. To his dismay, he learned the pools were closed in the winter. Apparently the apartment manager was of a like mind with Ivan's mother and brother. It was a shame, but given the mild temperatures, the water would have felt almost tepid.

He finished his shower, then stepped into the fur dryer provided by the gym, basking in the heat for as long as he could stand. This was a luxury few people in Russia could afford, and was one of many reasons why he did enjoy studying in America. When he felt like he was about to roast in his fur, he padded quietly to his locker, towel wrapped around his waist, and under his long, thick tail. He put on his hat and caught something moving out of the corner of his vision.

A bee flew at him, and would have hit him on the nose had he not stumbled back out of surprise. It buzzed around him, as if searching for a chance to sting him where he was most vulnerable. The towel fell to the floor as Ivan tried swatting the bee away, but it flew around his paws, avoiding the blows like a prize fighter in a championship bout.

Desperate, Ivan grabbed the towel from the floor and swung it blindly in front of him. He then saw the bee drop to the floor, its legs twitching, the wings buzzing once, then twice, then nothing. He never intended to kill it; he just wanted it to leave him alone.

"What's with all the racket, Ivan?" Tank stuck his head into the locker room, and Ivan hastily returned the towel around his waist.

"I was trying to stop bee from stinging me," Ivan said as he pointed at the floor where the bee lay.

Tank entered the room, smirking. "The bee's out..." His voice trailed off as his eyes caught the dead insect on the floor. "Huh. I guess we had an unregistered guest and didn't know about it." He grinned at Ivan. "What did you do to piss off the bee population?"

Ivan shook his head. "I do not know." He smiled weakly at Tank. "Perhaps they think I am silly old bear from children's book."

"Yeah, bees don't much like Winnie the Pooh."

Ivan stared at the bee, but it still had not moved since it last buzzed its wings. It was missing a leg and what seemed to be all of its right eye, though he wasn't certain. He was not willing to crouch down to look closer at it. He was satisfied he'd won the battle of snow leopard versus bumblebee.

"You really are scared of those bees," Tank said, grinning. "Don't worry, I'll sweep up the little bug and let you get dressed in a bee-free locker room."

Ivan murmured his thanks and the lapine departed. He collected his belongings from his locker and moved over to a secluded corner to get dressed. The bee was gone when he left the locker room. Tank was a lapine of his word, apparently. He was back behind the counter, and as Ivan signed out, Tank gave him a warm grin.

"Be careful of the nighttime bees, Ivan," he said.

Ivan merely smirked. "Bees do not come out at night."

"The bee in the locker room did."

Tank had a point, but it was one Ivan did not care to think about. Daytime bees were bad enough today, but ones at night? All he would hear would be the ominous buzz before the painful sting, followed by the allergic reaction.

"If I am stung, I hope you vill to be rescuing me."

Tank winked. "I'll be sure to do just that should a bee attack you outside the door, but when you vanish into the night, you're on your own." He then looked up at the clock hanging over his desk, then added "Of course, you could always run back here before we close at eleven."

"I vill remember that." Ivan said, then said his goodbyes and left the gym. The air was starting to cool down, which was fine for him. After he jogged to the apartment complex, he took off his tank top and paused to enjoy the cool air around his body. It felt wonderful, and rejuvenated his spirits a bit. The phone call to his family would be the perfect end to an otherwise dismal day.

After he entered the apartment he reached for the cordless phone on its cradle on the counter, but a slight movement from the aquarium caught his attention.

Cannon had her front paws on the glass and was staring at him with unblinking eyes.

Ivan blinked, all thoughts of the phone now forgotten as he returned Cannon's stare. He moved closer to the aquarium, then paused. "Hopper vill be happy you are not dead, Cannon."

Cannon flicked out her tongue in response.

"You gave him good scare." He felt silly for talking to Hopper's pet, but it had been a strange day. Iguanas who played dead. A bee that was determined to sting him. And a rabbit who flirted with him. Tank was the only person to do so since his arrival in the States.

Maybe this day was not as dismal as it started.

The iguana crept along the aquarium, tongue frequently flicking out. It was hard to believe before his workout, Ivan thought the iguana had died. The sight before him was very contrary to the fact. Cannon actively tried to climb the glass wall, even though her claws slipped on the glass. When Ivan approached the cordless phone, her attempts at scaling the wall increased. She almost seemed frustrated, and he thought he heard her hissing.

She had never been this active before. Perhaps her playing dead, then climbing the glass wall was an odd game for her. But Hopper's reaction was no game. He thought Cannon had died! Or was he playing some odd game as well? Was Eric in on the game?

He turned on the cordless, and was pleased to hear a dial tone. When he entered his bedroom he pulled out his international calling card and dialed the number to his family's phone in Russia. They would most certainly be awake.

It was one level of waiting after another--the clicks of the connection being made, the ringing of the phone. In fact, it rang so many times that he was about to hang up before he heard someone pick up. Instead of an immediate query phrased as a hello, he heard nothing but silence. Did the connection cut him off? He hesitated a moment before saying "Hello?"

A woman's voice replied. "Ivan?" His mother.

"Yes, mama." His heart leaped with joy at the sound of his mother's voice. They always spoke in English when he called, to keep him in the practice of speaking the language.

"Ivan, you are all right?"

The question was unusual, if only because she would usually gush for a minute or so before asking it. "Yes, mama. I am all right." Instinct prompted him to respond with "Are you all right?"

"*Nyet*. Something very tragic has happened. Your papa...your papa is dead."

Ivan suddenly felt cold, his fingers grew numb and it was only through sheer force of will that he kept his grip on the cordless. He sank, almost stumbled, into his desk chair. "Dead? Mama...how?"

"Son, do you remember vhat he brought home from Buyan?" There was no grief in her voice, only the steel of determination. The same determination that guided him to manhood. "Before he died, your papa sent it to you."

Ivan's thoughts were muddled in a mire of confusion. The tears would soon come, but first he had to know why. "Mama, how did papa die?" Ivan hadn't heard of his father succumbing to ill health. Was it an accident that took his life? Or was it something worse? He had many friends, but he also made his share of enemies.

"I am sorry, my son. I did not mean to burden you with the news, but...I think your father vould have vanted you to know. For your safety."

"My safety? Mama, vhat do you mean?"

"He vas murdered, and his murderer is coming for you."

"His murderer is coming for me?" Did he hear that correctly? His father's murderer was going to travel thousands of miles to murder him? "I velcome the chance to avenge my papa."

His mother choked off a sob, a heart-wrenching sound that made his heart sink. "No, son. Your papa would not vant you to be a killer, even to avenge him. This enemy...if vhat your papa said vas true, you vould be helpless." Static was starting to develop.

"Vhat did he tell you, mama?"

"For you to run if he finds you." There was a lengthy pause; Ivan heard his little brother's voice say something, but he could not make it out over the static. "Promise me you vill run, Ivan."

The static was getting worse. "Mama, vhat did Pitor say?" Somehow he felt it was important to know what his brother said. As if his life might just depend on it.

"He said you must not fight vhat killed your father."

Ivan shivered; though his fur was more than enough to keep him warm, this chill came from the very depths of his soul. "Vill you two be all right, mama?"

The static was now a raging storm, but he thought he heard the reply of yes. Or perhaps it was just his hope she said yes. He could not ask her to repeat herself, because a few seconds later, the phone went dead. No dial tone, and the power light was dark.

He muttered a curse, barely aware of the front door opening, followed by Hopper's voice.

"Cannon! You're alive!"

Ivan kept the door closed, leaning up against it and slowly sank towards the floor. His father was dead. A cruel twist of fate, swapping the iguana's place in the afterlife for his papa.

"Aw, baby! Who taught you to play dead, huh?" Hopper's voice grew louder as he heard the lapine run up to his door, rapidly knocking on it. Ivan! Are you there? Cannon's not dead!

Ivan did not respond. He could not share in Hopper's joy. It hurt him just to hear it in his voice; he would not ruin it by sharing his newly discovered tragedy. He would tell Hopper the news later. For now he would put on a brave front.

As he rose to his paws, he noticed something out of place on his desk. Next to the phone was an object that had not been there when he put the phone down. An egg lay there, its shell a perfect white, like the snow that blanketed his homeland in the winter.

It was the egg his father found on the island of Buyan twenty-three years ago. How did it get to America? Had it been delivered to him, and either Hopper or Eric opened the package without his consent? Even if that were true, Ivan was certain it had not been on the desk until now.

"Aw, you want out of your aquarium, Cannon? Okay."

Then Hopper started screaming.

CHAPTER 2

Ivan scrambled to his feet and almost ripped the door off its hinges when he opened it. He ran down the hallway and entered the living room, and froze in fear when he saw the reason for Hopper's screams.

Cannon was thrashing about in Hopper's grip, her jaws clamped down on his eyebrow, clawing at his face. Hopper was on his knees, trying in vain to pull her off of him. "IVAN! Fuck, man! Help me! She's trying to gouge my eye out!"

Ivan stepped forward, but hesitated. The blood dripping down Hopper's cheek...the color so vibrant; it made both the room seem brighter and him feel light headed. He had to force himself to take deep breaths before he started hyperventilating.

"God dammit, Ivan! Fucking help me!"

He lurched towards Hopper and grabbed the iguana with both paws. She resisted his efforts at removal, since he was trying his best not to hurt Hopper. "She von't let go!"

"Come on, man! You're a fucking Hercules! Pull this bitch off of me!"

"I do not vant to hurt you!"

"She's *killing* me, man! Pull this bitch off of--"

Cannon ripped some flesh from Hopper's eyebrow, and some of his blood splattered on Ivan's face. He fell to the floor, his grip on Cannon lost. He heard the iguana fall to the floor with a heavy thump, and for a moment feared he would be attacked next. After wiping the blood away from his face, he frantically searched the area for the suddenly murderous pet, and found her laying on her side, her lifeless eyes staring at the wall. She hadn't moved, but he still kept his distance.

She had played dead before.

He moved over to crouch beside Hopper. The bleeding had already stopped, and this worried Ivan--shouldn't Hopper still be bleeding from such a terrible wound? Iguanas had sharp, serrated teeth; being bitten by one was like being slashed with glass. Hopper was also staring off into the distance, eyes wide open. Was he in shock? "Hopper?"

"Get...some ice..."

Ice would help stem the blood flow in normal circumstances, but this... "All right, I vill." Ivan rose to his paws, moving towards the kitchen. He grabbed all the ice trays in the refrigerator and put as many as he could into a plastic sandwich bag, zipping it shut. "Ve need to put this on your wound," he said as he turned to face Hopper...

...who was no longer there. He had vanished.

"Hopper?" Where had he gone? He crept forward, an uneasy feeling building in his stomach. Was this an elaborate prank, perhaps inspired by that celebrity and his televised pranks on other celebrities? Hopper loved watching it. Maybe Ivan was being set up for one.

No. The fear and pain in Hopper's eyes when Cannon had her teeth in his flesh were real. The wound was real. The blood was far too real.

But where had he gone?

"Hopper?" Ivan called out into the empty room.

<Behind you.>

Ivan knew he would see Hopper when he turned around, but the sight of him standing there unsettled him. Something was wrong, but the stress and confusion from the events of the last few minutes left his brain in shock.

<You have something that belongs to me, little kitten,> Hopper growled.

Little kitten? Hopper was almost a foot and a half shorter than him, but Ivan found any protests dying in his throat before he could utter them. Something was terribly *wrong* about Hopper, and he struggled to put the pieces together for an answer.

<Give it to me,> Hopper lifted his arm, palm upwards, fingers curled in a mimicry of a claw.

Ivan stepped back, his tail lashing around behind his back. He barely felt it strike the aquarium where Hopper(?) kept his former pet. Cannon was still lifeless on the floor, but he kept away from her nonetheless.

Hopper stepped forward, his lips pulled back into a snarl. His eyes seemed darker, as if a light behind them was dimming. <Give it to me *now!*>

It then clicked. Hopper was speaking perfectly accented Russian when before his knowledge of the language was limited to *da, nyet,* and *comrade.* He never had the heart to tell Hopper that the latter was not a word found in Russian.

<Give what to you?> he said, unconsciously lapsing into his native tongue.

<I want what your father stole from me. Give me the egg. I know you have it.>

Ivan swallowed the lump trying to form in his throat. <It is in my bedroom. Take it. Go away.>

Hopper, or whatever was posing as Hopper, emitted a raspy chuckle in which the lapine could never duplicate in life. <No, little kitten,> he said with a shake of his head. <You will get it for me. You will place it in this paw and then I will leave you to mourn for your deceased father.> His eyes were now darkening into pools of midnight. <If you do not...> his words trailed away as he glanced at Cannon.

To Ivan's horror, Cannon was rising to her feet again, but she was undergoing an inner transformation. Her bones cracked as they shifted into new positions, allowing her to stand up on her hind legs. Her shoulders broadened, and she *grinned* up at Ivan. He could feel the unearthly hate in her gaze, and could not withhold the mewl that escaped his throat. <W-what are you?> he asked the thing that was once Hopper.

The question seemed to surprise him; his eyes widened in disbelief. <You do not know? Did they not teach you cubs anything?> He shook his head, almost sadly. <I did you a favor, it seems, killing your father. He should not leave you ignorant of the true history of the old country.>

A shiver of realization washed over Ivan. <You killed my father.>

<Yes.>

Ivan remembered his mother's words:
Promise me you vill run.

Ivan ran past Hopper towards the front door.

<You vould run, eh?> said the thing who was once Hopper as Ivan hurriedly opened the door and entered the cool night. The darkness seemed oppressive, as if there would be no safety found in its depths. The exterior apartment lighting was too bright. Running seemed futile. Hopeless.

Ivan ran as fast as his legs could take him regardless.

A screech came from behind him, from the apartment he just fled. He knew the transformed Cannon would chase him, but he hoped it would not prove to be faster than him. As he ran towards a dumpster, Ivan almost passed it, then realized the garbage there might mask his scent. Could iguanas track by scent? Perhaps not, but this new form of Cannon might have the ability.

There were two dumpsters in a granite enclosure. He squeezed in between the two and ducked down, curling up his tail in front of him. If Cannon could track his scent through the smell of garbage within the dumpsters, he would be in trouble. If the Once Hopper went looking for him, he would be in fatal trouble. This thing murdered his father. Ivan had no hopes he could overcome such an enemy.

Another screech, but this one died down into a low growl, followed by a quiet hiss. Cannon was near. Unnervingly so. He thought he saw its shadow cast from the fluorescent bulbs on the awning above. The shadow looked too big for such a small creature, but perhaps that was from the illusion of size shadows sometimes cast.

Then Cannon came into sight. She was several feet away, but the shadow she had cast was perfect for her. Her size had increased. While he couldn't make out too many details, he could see those claws and those teeth. Those sharp, deadly teeth.

She hadn't seem him yet, and he tried to scrunch himself deeper between the dumpsters. She swept her head around, and for a moment he thought his movement had exposed him to her. She continued her sweep, then moved forward until she was out of sight. Ivan released a quiet sigh of relief.

What to do now, though? Stay there until he was certain he could slip away? And then where would he go? Who could he trust with his dilemma? There was a Bullseye retail store next to the apartments, but would anyone in there believe him? He was certain they would call the police, and he was not sure the American police were any better than their Russian counterparts.

Then he remembered something Tank said at the gym:

Of course, you could always run back here before we close at eleven.

Ivan had no logical reason to believe Tank would truly assist him, nor was he certain the rabbit would *believe* him. For all he knew, Tank would throw him out of the gym and leave him to the cruel fate of whatever the Once Hopper had in mind.

Still, was there any other choice?

Ivan sat there, his body rigid with tension. There, between the two dumpsters, he wondered if he should dare to sneak out from his hiding spot and run for it. He was in excellent shape, but he was no runner. Jogging was effortless, but could he outrun the monster that was once Cannon? When she was small, he would have harbored no doubts whatsoever, but what if she'd grown in the minutes he'd seen her?

He felt his heart thudding against his ribcage. The thumps felt as powerful as a heavyweight boxer's blows. Just the thought of being caught by the monstrous Cannon was enough to frizz out his fur. How long had he waited between the dumpsters? A few minutes? An hour? He didn't have a watch. The flow of time seemed to stretch out into infinity.

Genesis '0?

Something had to be done; if he remained in his hiding place, he would be found. If not by Cannon, then perhaps by the Once Hopper. Neither fate was desirable. He would have to make his way carefully and quietly. His gray fur would betray him, as it stood out in the darkness. Why could he not be in the snowfall of Siberia? At least then the cold would slow down the Once Cannon. Or maybe not--perhaps the power which granted her the ability to walk upright and the increase in size also gave her a resistance to the cold.

Something still needed to be done. Inaction would only lead him to his doom. Ivan slipped away from his hidey hole, looking left and right for any signs of the Once Cannon. He saw no signs of her, nor did he hear any telltale sounds which could give away her location. This did not make him feel any safer. Around every corner, she might be laying in wait. Every shadow could be concealing her from sight.

He ran towards the Bullseye store, wincing with every click of toe claws against the concrete sidewalk. His eyes darted at every movement both real and imagined. And there were so many of the latter. A leaf drifting by startled him. The wind which blew against his fur chilled him on a spiritual level, as if it were the breath of Death itself.

Ivan had wanted to fight his father's killer, but instead he chose the path of escape. He felt cowardly, afraid to sacrifice his own life to avenge his father's.

But there was Hopper to think about. Was he gone? Was his life snuffed out when the thing possessed his body? Could Ivan save his friend as well as avenge his father, or would he be avenging two lives?

Ivan's thoughts suddenly focused on Eric. Where was he? Was he all right? What would happen if he came home and the Once Hopper was still--

A shriek from above the Bullseye store interrupted his thoughts. Crouched on the roof like some demonic gargoyle was the Once Cannon.

It had been waiting for him.

Ivan froze at the sight of the Once Cannon leering down at him until it started scaling down the wall like a spider. Its claws sank into the bricks like a spoon into frozen ice cream; the progress was slow, but when Ivan ran past it and around the corner of the building, his ears picked up the sound of its increased descent.

It was playing with him. Mocking him. *I can catch you anytime I want*, its actions told Ivan, *but first we will play.*

Ivan hoped he would prove to be a very poor player. He moved with an increased, frantic pace. The parking lot of the Bullseye was empty--he must have remained hidden between the dumpsters for hours after all. A hurried glance past the entrance doors showed only darkness. No one would be in there. He had a hope, however slim, that he might have been able to find shelter inside.

He moved faster, fearful that if he slowed down, or looked over his shoulder, the Once Cannon would be leering scant inches behind him. The unearthly shriek of his pursuer did sound closer now. It was gaining, and he already felt himself getting a stitch in his side. He was not built for running, but running was the only thing that could save his life.

He had almost reached the street that separated the Bullseye parking lot from the gym's when he saw Tank locking up. There was no mistaking that large figure which gave him his nickname, and for a moment his heart leaped with joy, giving him the second wind he so desperately needed. The stitch in his side was gone and his feet seemed to fly across the parking lot, the streetlamps blurring past him. Did he feel the air behind him part, as if from a swipe of claws?

Ivan *knew* the thing was behind him now, as the absence of shrieks were paradoxically deafening to his ears. Fear brought out the will for more speed. He had never run so fast for so long before. He would pay for it later...if he survived. It would be a price he would gladly pay if he lived.

But first he would have to reach Tank before--

The parking lot suddenly ended and Ivan stumbled off the curb, his arms windmilling to help him keep his balance as he raced across the street. Somehow he kept himself from falling as he reached the gym's parking lot and Tank.

"Ivan?" Tank looked at him as he walked down the steps, casually tossing his keyring into the air and catching it. He paused in mid step, cocking his head. "What the hell's wrong?" He narrowed his eyes as Ivan quickly grew nearer to the steps. "Is that blood on your--"

"Tank! Please! You must help me!"

Tank's eyes widened as he looked past Ivan. "Behind you!"

The warning came too late as something slammed against Ivan from behind, the weight bringing him down.

Ivan expected the claws to wrap around his throat and either choke him or rip into his flesh. Instead Tank reached down to grab at his hand, pulling him up to his feet. "Come on!" the rabbit said as he starting running towards the parking lot. "It's not going to stay down for long!"

The snow leopard was slow to follow, so Tank simply dragged him along for a second before instinct took hold of Ivan's legs, and he started to run. The adrenaline was still coursing through his system, but it would not last for much longer. "Vh-vhat happened?"

Tank reached a blue GMC truck that was parked in a remote spot away from the gym. It suddenly roared into life when he pressed on a remote attached to his keyring and briefly chirped once as he pressed the remote again.

Tank opened the door in a rush. "Hurry, get in!" he said as he followed his own advice.

Ivan looked over his shoulder as he entered the truck. The Once Cannon was already rushing towards them, and in the fluorescent lighting of the streetlamps, there was no question she...*it*...was larger. Almost equal to his own seven foot height. But where he was bulky, it was lean--moving so lightning quick Ivan expected it to grab the door and prevent him from closing it.

It didn't happen; Ivan quickly slammed the door shut as the truck sped forward, going over the curb and onto the street. They were already on Sparks Avenue moving quickly towards I-80 when the snow leopard looked behind him for any signs of pursuit. The darkness prevented him from seeing clearly, but there seemed to be no sign of the Once Cannon.

"I think we lost it, whatever the hell it is," Tank said as he glanced in the rear view mirror.

"Vhat happened? It tackled me at parking lot, but..." Ivan was starting to feel exhausted as the adrenalin left his system.

"I drop-kicked the freak after it knocked you down." Tank glanced at Ivan, and a guilty look crossed his face. "I should have moved faster, but you kinda freaked me out with the blood on your face. I'm sorry for that, but it won't happen again."

Again? Ivan hoped that was the last he would ever see of the Once Cannon, but some voice inside his head whispered a different thought. It would find him, and perhaps not even Tank's strength could stop it in their next encounter. The Once Cannon was changing rapidly. Growing in size, speed, and what else? Perhaps strength. Perhaps intelligence? It definitely had no lack of cunning, since it had known he would be moving towards the Bullseye.

"So you mind telling me what the hell that thing was?"

"It vas my roommate's pet." Ivan hoped Tank would believe him. He certainly would not have, had it not happened to him personally!

"Your roomie has a deadly taste in pets. Next time maybe he should just adopt an alligator."

Ivan stared at Tank for a moment before he spoke. "How did you know my roommate is male?"

Tank kept his eyes on the road ahead. "You don't seem the type to have a female roomie. Now, what the hell was that thing back there, and why do you look like the survivor of a horror film?"

Ivan certainly felt like a horror victim. He still hurt all over from falling on the asphalt, and he could only imagine how his face looked with the dried blood. "It is long story. I am confused by many parts of it."

"Just try me, Ivan," Tank said as he stopped at a red light. Ivan almost wanted to scream at him to keep on going, but certainly they were far away enough from the Once Cannon that they could afford this brief pause.

So Ivan told Tank the bare bones of the story, realizing that details wouldn't help a skeptic believe his tale anyway. The lapine didn't interrupt with any questions during Ivan's story, nor did he look at the snow leopard. When the light turned green, Tank eased the truck forward, getting into the turn lane for I-80 West and continued to listen.

"So your roomie is possessed."

"*Da.*"

"And he wants this egg that somehow appeared in your bedroom."

"*Da.*"

"This egg was in Russia before."

"Yes." Ivan wished Tank would stop asking questions he clearly knew the answer to, but he kept silent on the matter. The rabbit saved his life. He owed him.

"I think this problem is bigger than what I can handle." Tank glanced at Ivan as they merged onto the freeway. "We gotta get some help."

Ivan felt gratitude swell in his heart. Tank was going to help him. There was hope after all. "Vhere are we going?"

"First of all, I gotta call two guys I know. They're brothers. You'd like them if the circumstances weren't so drastic."

Ivan's ears twitched. "Drastic?"

Tank nodded. "Yeah, this thing that possessed your roomie and turned the dead pet into a monster...you don't think that's the limit of its power, do you? Who says it can't do more stuff?"

Ivan had not considered it in his haste to escape the monster. "So I am still in danger?"

"Not just you, Ivan. I helped you out, so I might as well assume I'm in trouble with you." He reached over to pat the snow leopard's thigh. "But you couldn't have picked a better guy to help you. I got rabbit's feet, and you know how lucky they are, right? After all, they got that monster off your back?" He winked over at Ivan and grinned widely.

Ivan looked away, watching the lights of Reno grow closer. "I did not mean to put you in danger."

"I know you didn't, but I'm not the type to turn people away when they need help."

Ivan's reply was swallowed up by an unearthly shriek behind them.

"Shit!" Tank glanced at the rear view mirror. "How did it catch up with us?"

Ivan looked over his shoulder and found the Once Cannon's eyes on him. They were glowing a dull red, and he could see the ridge of horns along its eye ridges. It slapped its open palm on the rear window, and looked surprised that the glass did not shatter. It unleashed an unholy shriek as it balled up those long clawed fingers and repeatedly pummeled against the glass.

Tank laughed. "I think our little monster's getting frustrated."

"Vhy is glass not shattering?" Ivan asked as he shied away from the rear window as best he could.

"ALON ceramic. Transparent armor. They use it in tanks." The truck suddenly accelerated as they approached the Rock Boulevard exit. "Lean up against your door!"

Ivan did as he was told, but his hands also went for the dashboard, his claws sliding out as they gripped the edge. The truck barreled down the exit ramp towards the intersection. The light was against them; the red glow baleful to Ivan's eyes.

Tank wrenched the steering wheel to the right, the truck screeching around the corner so sharply that for a second it rode on just two wheels. Then it crashed back down to all four and sped towards the intersection of Rock and Prater.

Ivan found himself struggling to catch his breath. "You are crazy driver!"

"Tell me something my driving instructor never told me, or better yet, how about seeing if it's still back there?"

Ivan stole a glance, and even in the darkness he knew the Once Cannon was no longer there. It must have been dislodged from the sharp turn. The snow leopard slumped against the seat, closing his eyes as relief flooded his system. "It is gone."

"I'll believe you if it doesn't attack in the next five minutes." Still, Tank slowed down the truck as he turned north down Prater Avenue. "I think I know what happened."

Ivan opened his eyes to look over his shoulder and into the darkness again. "It hid behind bed, vhere ve could not see?"

Tank nodded grimly. "Exactly. Clever little freak, ain't it? Whoever did that mojo to it must have knocked it up a few rungs on the ol' evolutionary ladder." He met Ivan's gaze for a second before turning back to watching the road ahead. "And it's a continual climb up said ladder. Freak's bigger now, more dangerous. We're going to need some big help to get rid of it and its master."

"You are very calm."

"No sense in losing it. That'll just get us both killed."

"You should be monster hunter instead of vorking at gym."

Tank grinned. "Oh, the gym is just for tax purposes. My real job is saving innocent people from the terrors that try to disrupt the natural order of things."

Ivan's eyes widened some. "You are kidding."

"Yeah, I was kidding."

"Good."

"I only save innocent people part-time. Like tonight, for example."

Ivan squinted at Tank. "So you have encountered such things before?"

"Not anything like what we just got rid of, no, but I've seen some things that'll make your spots turn white." Tank grew quiet for a moment, then said, "That would be an awesome look for you, you know."

"I am surprised my fur is not already vhite after all that has happened."

"Aw, come on. You're a lot stronger than you give yourself credit for. I've seen people break down over trifling stuff, like their computer dying on them. You're scared, sure, but you've still got it together."

Ivan looked down at his hands. "I do not feel like I have it together."

"Then you sure do hide it pretty damn good," Tank said with a sidelong grin plastered on his muzzle.

Ivan raised his hands to his face. They were steady, without a tremor in sight. He had expected them to be shaking nervously. As he balled up his hands into fists and returned them to his lap, he murmured "Perhaps you are right."

Tank smirked. "Of course I'm right."

"How are you so sure of yourself?"

"I blame my parents." Tank said.

"Vhat are they like?"

Tank shook his head, the grin still on his face. "I'll tell you later when this is all over, or maybe I'll just introduce you to them. Mom's gonna love you."

When, not if. Tank's confidence was infectious, but Ivan still harbored doubts. What would the Once Cannon be like during their next encounter? He could still see those demonic features in his mind's eye. Where once there was a dull look to Cannon's eyes, the Once Cannon had a crafty intelligence to them. "I...I miss Poppa."

"You loved him a lot, didn't you?" Tank asked quietly.

Ivan nodded as his vision blurred with tears that stung as they trailed down his cheeks. "I c-cannot believe I vill not see him again." He closed his eyes, wiping away the tears with the back of his paw.

The weight of Tank's arm spread out along his shoulders before the lapine rubbed the side of the snow leopard's head. "It's okay," Tank whispered, "just let it all out. I'm here. I won't leave you."

Ivan buried his head against Tank's shoulder, his paws clutching against Tank's side as he released the tears that had been building up since he had learned of his poppa's murder. There was nothing he could do about that. His poppa was gone. Ivan prayed it was a painless death, but doubt darkened his thoughts.

He pushed the doubts and thoughts of his poppa to the side. He had to live in the now, which dealt with surviving the monster which pursued him, and, with luck, defeat it. Then he could deal with the Once Hopper, and avenge his poppa.

To do that, he would have to deal with the Once Cannon.

And if he were to die in the process, he could die knowing he tried his best.

Tank drove the truck into a Sav-Mart gas station. "Stay inside the truck while I make sure your pet monster isn't here," Tank said as he opened the door. He paused, ears swiveling around while he peered into the darkness. The parking lot was well lit, but one bulb dimly flickered, ready to go out at any moment.

What if the Once Cannon could emerge from the darkness caused by a burnt out street lamp? It would then attack Tank, who would be caught unaware, and slice his flesh open with its razor sharp talons. Then as he would watch his lapine savior fall, it would come for him. The glass would no longer an obstacle to its increased power. It would shatter the barrier that kept it from Ivan, and--

Tank rapped on the driver's side window. "It's safe. Come on, let's grab some essentials."

Ivan welcomed the interruption of his dire scenario. Certainly not even the Once Cannon could bring down Tank, who lived up to his name. He seemed unstoppable, and could adapt to situations quickly. Unlike himself, Tank could bring down the monster, and do it with *style*.

As he followed Tank inside, he took one final glance at the darkness that surrounded him. Did he hear a distant cry? Maybe it was the wind... only the air was still.

"Ivan? You shouldn't be outside," Tank said. "This kind of neighborhood isn't the friendliest one to be alone in."

Ivan scampered inside, rubbing his face with both hands. Flecks of dried blood spotted his fingers. "I should go to restroom," he said.

"Good idea. I'll pick up some energy drinks and some beef jerky. We might need it to keep up our momentum."

The restroom was recently cleaned, and the sting of bleach which filled Ivan's nostrils was so strong it forced him to breath through his mouth. It was a small price to pay to get cleaned up. His facial fur was speckled with dried blood, so he dampened a paper towel in the sink and was able to wipe it all away. It improved his appearance, and he mustered up a small smile to his reflection.

"Everything vill be all right," his reflection 'said', and he almost believed it.

Tank was at the register, his purchases already in a bag except for a tall energy drink in his hand. Ivan could make out the label "Creature". A picture of a fierce wolf sliced at the logo. "It just feels right," Tank said as he caught Ivan's questioning look. As he moved towards the entrance, he retrieved a red ball cap from the bag. "Here, I thought you might want a replacement."

Ivan had forgotten he had not worn his old cap since the start of his dreadful adventure. "Th-thank you," he said as he put it on.

"No problem, Ivan," Tank said as he got into the truck. "It looked weird, you going without a cap."

Maybe Fate was trying to tell him something...

Everything will be all right.

"Too bad they didn't have any shirts in your size," Tank said as they pulled out of the parking lot and into the darkened street, "because they had some nice ones...well, for convenience stores."

Ivan fingered the brim of his new hat. "The cap is enough, Tank. Thank you again for it." None of his friends in America had ever bought him anything. Except Hopper, who bought him lunch. As he recalled the memory of his smiling face, Ivan felt the pang of loss. It was almost as great as the loss of his poppa. Hopper had done his best to make sure Ivan was comfortable during orientation. It was his idea to room together with Eric, and it had worked out up until...

"You thinking about your poppa?"

Ivan slowly shook his head, keeping his eyes on the road ahead, as if some sort of co-pilot. "*Nyet.* I am thinking of my roommate. Do you..." Ivan's question died on his lips, unspoken. Did he really want the answer?

Would it be better to just focus on the matter at hand and hope Hopper could be restored?

"He's going to be fine, Ivan. I bet that guy's got a lot of good karma he can cash in."

"How do you know?"

"I just have faith, and I know some things you don't. I've seen things, remember?" Before Ivan could reply, he suddenly heard wind chimes coming from Tank's pocket. "Someone left me voice mail. I'll listen to it when we get to the twins. I tried calling them, but their phone's been disconnected again." He chuckled at that. "Not very organized, the twins."

"What if it is important?"

Tank shrugged. "I'm sure it is. Otherwise they wouldn't have left voice mail, but right now you're more important."

Ivan felt a wave of emotion wash over him. This rabbit barely knew him, and yet he was risking his life for him. Would he do the same for Tank? As he watched the lapine calmly drive the truck, he thought--no, he *knew*--he would. A bond was forming between the two, and hopefully they would survive this trial so that they could continue to develop it. "You are good Samaritan."

"Didn't we go over this one already? I'm just a rabbit. What kind of person would I be if I'd just let the monster have at you back at the gym's parking lot, huh?" He didn't wait for Ivan's reply. "A damned piss-poor one."

Ivan felt the smile on his muzzle. It seemed to warm him, encourage him. "You are good Samaritan." The thought of the Once Cannon catching up to him no longer held him captive with terror. Of course, the situation might change when they *did* face it again, but Tank would not abandon him. He knew this as fact. And he would not abandon Tank either.

"We're almost there. They live above a soup kitchen in downtown Reno. Own it themselves, and--"

The truck suddenly skidded across the lane as something crashed into it. As the tires squealed, they were joined by an unearthly shriek.

Another shriek accompanied it.

"Ivan?" Tank's voice sounded shaken, but not weak. "Are you okay?"

Ivan, on the other hand, felt weak. He had hit his head on the window during the impact, and now the pain crept in behind his eyes. "*Nyet*, but I will manage."

A car had smashed into the passenger side of the truck. The driver was slumped against the steering wheel, unconscious or perhaps worse.

"Alright, we got to get out of here," Tank said.

Ivan kept his eyes on the driver. "But driver may be hurt."

Tank looked over at Ivan as if the snow leopard might be transforming into another species. "You did hear the double shrieks out there, right? Your pet monster has a friend now, and both of them are coming after us."

The driver started to get out of the car; his movements were slow, as if he had sustained injuries from the impact. "He is hurt. Ve should not leave him alone."

"Ivan, I can't take anymore strays with me. You and me, we're not small guys, and that guy that hit my truck and thus increased my insurance payments doesn't look like he's small either."

The driver was overweight, his belly bulging from behind the button-down dress shirt and coat he was wearing. He rubbed the back of his head, as if in pain. "Ve cannot leave him."

"No, we *can* leave him and we *should* leave him." Tank put the truck into gear. "And guess what? We *are* going to leave him."

As the truck moved forward and away from the crash, Ivan unbuckled his seat belt and shoved the door open, hopping out of the vehicle.

"Ivan! What the hell are you doing?"

Ivan had no idea, but he ran towards the driver, ignoring the pain which thumped inside his skull. He could not leave this man in jeopardy. He would never be able to sleep at night with the knowledge that he did not at least try to save an innocent.

"God dammit, Ivan! Get back in the truck!"

Ivan ignored Tank's demands. He had to at least warn the driver of the impending danger. He stopped just out of reach of the driver, who was bent forward as if trying to catch his breath. "Sir? Are you all right?"

Another unearthly shriek echoed in the distance. It sounded as if it were coming from somewhere close, but with all the buildings downtown, it was difficult to judge. Ivan knew he was losing precious time.

"Ivan, don't make me come out there and drag your spotted ass back in the truck!"

"Sir, please. It is not safe to be here. You must leave quickly." Ivan took a step back. He had given the warning. Now he could flee.

This time, the shriek he heard was right in front of him.

The driver looked up, his eyes red like blood and his muzzle split open into a grin far too wide to still be considered anything but a monster.

It shrieked at Ivan before it lunged at him.

Ivan stumbled back, which saved him from being knocked down as the monster landed where he once stood. The Once Pug's teeth fell onto the road, and to Ivan's horror he could see new ones growing in. Jagged daggers that dripped a greenish goo. Acid? Venom? Whatever it was, Ivan had no desire to find out. He backed away towards Tank's truck. So very close, but if he turned around...

The thing jumped towards him, and Ivan instinctively swung his arm to defend himself. It shrieked, and Ivan was surprised to see it was cupping its cheek. He could barely make out the blood welling up between its fingers.

"Ivan! Look out!"

When Ivan saw the Once Cannon emerge from an alleyway, he turned to run towards the truck. His heart was racing faster than him, but he managed to get into the truck just as Tank stepped on the gas. Ivan scrambled to get in, shutting the door behind him, somehow managing to keep from slamming it against his tail.

Ivan looked behind him. The Once Cannon and the Once Pug were both gone. Vanished into the night.

"I'm not going to say it," Tank said, his voice in a hushed growl. He was shaking, but from anger over Ivan's actions or fear for Ivan's life, the snow leopard could not say.

Ivan, however, knew what Tank did not want to tell him. "Go ahead," he said, trying to catch his breath as he put on his seat belt across his chest. "I deserve it."

"All right, then. What you did was stupid and risky. You could have been killed."

"I vas hoping for something like they say on television."

"Like 'I told you so'?"

"*Da.*"

"Tough luck, kitty. I don't watch television." Tank's expression then softened as he relaxed, the truck slowing down to safer speeds. "Still, I can't fault you too much for your big heart."

Hearing that lightened Ivan's spirits, but when he looked at his paws, he discovered his claws were out, and they were wet with blood. The Once Pug's blood. He hissed as he drew in a sharp intake of breath.

"Ivan? What's wrong?"

"I...I bled thing."

"You're bleeding?" The truck screeched to a halt before Tank grabbed Ivan's hands, searching for signs of injury.

Ivan pulled his hands away from Tank. "No! I...I cut monster. Vith claws."

"Oh. Good for you."

"I...I have never used claws before on anyone." His stomach slowly churned, and he started to roll down the window.

"Ivan, what're you--"

Tank's words were drowned out by Ivan's stomach emptying itself onto the road, followed by the dry heaves when it had nothing else to lose.

"--forget I asked," Tank said when Ivan turned away from the window, leaning forward to tuck his head as close between his legs as the seat belt would provide.

"May I have vater?" Ivan rasped.

"Sure thing, and we're almost at the soup kitchen."

"Vill they help us?"

"Won't know until we get there."

Ivan's heart sank into a pit of fear. "But you said ve were going to get help."

Tank gave a slight nod of his head. "I also said we were going to these guys first. They know where we need to go." He turned left, down North Virginia street. They passed the three major casinos, all linked together: The Carnival Carnival, the Golden Regency, and the El Diego. At the final one, Tank drove the truck into the parking garage. "Vhy are ve going here?"

"Because the twins live close by, and I don't want to have our monsters find my truck. It's been damaged enough for one night." As Tank found a spot to park the vehicle, he frowned. "So you think that pug guy was already a monster when he hit us?"

Ivan had not considered it. "I thought it vas accident that killed him, and then he became monster."

Tank got out of the truck. "I doubt the accident killed him. I bet he had a heart attack or something."

They took the stairs down to the street. Tank kept his eyes in front, while Ivan glanced nervously around until the lapine placed a hand on his shoulder. "Relax, Ivan. You look this nervous, we might get mugged."

Ivan looked up at Tank with wide-eyed alarm. "Is it that dangerous here?"

"Compared to being chased by a monster? Probably not. And come to think of it, I don't think anyone would mug us. Well, you they might mug if you keep on acting skittish." Tank gave Ivan's shoulder a friendly rub. "So come on, act like you're not afraid of anything."

Ivan rubbed his shoulder once Tank's hand left it. "But I vould be lying. I am afraid. For me and for you."

A deep chuckle slipped out of Tank's throat. "You're a sweet guy, Ivan, and it takes someone who's brave to admit fear."

Ivan blinked. "Is that not contradictory?"

"People are full of contradictions. They go to war in the name of peace. Parents spank their children and tell them not to hurt anyone smaller than them. They vote for someone who offers them hope and criticizes him the minute he tries to change things." Tank chuckled again. "So yeah, it's contradictory, but that's one reason why I love this crazy life." He suddenly thrust a finger across the street at a two story building nestled between a condemned motel and a dilapidated movie theater. A sign above the doors proclaimed it to be the *Soup Kitchen for Wayward Ponies*. "There we are."

There were no lights on inside the first floor, but there was a single window lit up above it. Before Tank could cross the street, Ivan grabbed his wrist.

"Can they help us? Vill they help us?"

Tank paused, looking into Ivan's eyes. Whatever he saw made him purse his lips, followed by him cupping Ivan's cheek.

"I don't know, Ivan, but I'm going to help you all the way through this."

CHAPTER 3

Tank and Ivan crossed the street, both of them watching for possible incoming traffic (though Ivan was on the lookout for things with claws and teeth). There was an intercom set next to the door, and Tank stabbed the button with his thumb. A few seconds later, seconds which were filled with Ivan constantly glancing around despite Tank's advice, the intercom crackled to life.

"Hello?"

"Brent, it's Tank. Lemme in, please."

"Sure thing, Tank. I'll send my brother down in a second."

The darkness seemed to close in on Ivan, the slightest noise caused him to flinch before Tank placed a hand on his shoulder. "Relax, Ivan."

"It is hard to."

Tank was quiet for a moment. "Yeah. I know."

The lights came on downstairs, and the door opened. A horse stood there, his dark chestnut brown coat gleaming in the artificial light. He wore his mane in a long, thick braid. "Hey, Tank," the horse smiled, showing a row of flat teeth. He looked up at both them, but his gaze lingered on Ivan. "Who's your spotty friend?"

"Brooks, this is Ivan. He needs my help."

"Hi, Ivan. How about you two come on in? You don't mind me saying so, but you both look kind of frazzled."

Ivan looked over at Tank, who seemed as confident and calm as when he was in the gym's parking lot. Frazzled? Ivan knew he was ten times as frazzled-looking as Tank.

The area looked like a cafeteria. The walls were of a muted blue color;

DEATHLESS

Ivan almost thought them to be gray. Rows of picnic tables lined the floor, and there was a food line at the far back of the room. "What kind of help do you need?" Brooks asked as he led them to the kitchen area.

"I'll tell you when we see Brent."

"That bad?"

"I'll tell you when--"

Brooks waved off the comment. "Geez, it must be bad if you're acting stubborn like your dad."

Tank shrugged. "For my dad, it's not an act."

The mention of Tank's dad sent a pang through Ivan's heart. Tank, at least, still had a father. "Tank said you vould help."

Brooks glanced over his shoulder, his grin transformed into a full-blow smile. "That is a kick-ass accent...Ivan, was it? Where you from, big guy?"

"From Russia."

Brooks opened a door, revealing a stairwell going up to the second floor. "Neat. Always did want to visit there. Lots of folklore and history, even if it does get freakin' cold over there. I just hope we can help you, big guy."

Ivan had no response for that. He wanted to be in familiar territory and not in this city, which now seemed very alien and dangerous to him. He simply nodded, which Brooks seemed to accept as he clopped up the flight of stairs ahead of them.

Tank, who took up the rear, reached over to rub Ivan's shoulders. "We're going to make it."

Ivan wished he had Tank's confidence.

The second floor was a studio apartment. Ivan could see a bed, a kitchen, and a living room with a large flat screen television mounted on

Graveyard Greg

one wall. Behind the sofa the windows showed off the view of the Sierras, though they were hidden away by the night. Seated on one of two sofas was the other twin, Brent. They looked identical, but where Brooks had his mane done up in a long braid, Brent had his styled in a mohawk. Not just any mohawk, though. Where most were thin, his was thick and broad. Ivan idly wondered how much hairspray or styling gel it took to keep such a monumental hairstyle.

"Who's your friend, Tank?" Brent asked as he stood up. They even sounded alike, but fortunately the hairstyles and different colored shorts (Brooks wore a pair of black shorts whereas Brent wore blue) kept the confusion to nil.

"This is Ivan. Ivan, this is Brent."

Brent extended his hand. "Pleased to meet you, Ivan." He even had the same charming smile as his brother.

"Thank you for letting us in your home."

"Oh my. He *is* from Russia." Brent looked over at his twin. "You weren't--"

"--bullshitting you? Of course I wasn't." Brooks took a pair of sunglasses from the coffee table in front of the sofa and put them on. "That would be, like--"

"--totally rude. Yeah, I agree." Brent went over and sat on the sofa, putting on the second pair of sunglasses. "Have a seat, guys--"

"--the sofa's very comfortable," Brooks said, sitting beside his brother, leaning on him.

Ivan felt dizzy as the two completed each other's sentences. When did Brooks tell his brother where he was from? He looked to Tank for assistance, and Tank mouthed the words *I'll tell you later.*

"Oh, go on, Tank. Tell him," Brooks said, smiling. "We don't want him--"

"--to think we're odd," Brent said.

"Even though we are," Brooks continued, nodding his head.

"Total agreement," Brent agreed with a similar nod.

"I'd love to tell him, but it'll have to wait," Tank said, his tone a bit gruff. "I need to know where Jolly is."

Brooks and Brent's eyebrows both raised simultaneously. "You're going--"

"--on a pilgrimage?" Brent asked.

"I have to. Jolly's got the safe house. The faster we're out of here, the safer you two are."

Brent frowned. "How bad is it? Are you going--"

"--to be all right? We can help. We have--"

"--our own special talents."

Tank shook his head. "I'm risking too much already. Just tell us where to find Jolly, and maybe lend us your Mustang. I parked my truck at the El Diego."

"It must be bad--"

"--if you're trusting casino parking," Brooks said.

"It's bad. Life-threatening even, since--" Tank's words were cut off as suddenly there was a thud down below, as if something heavy hit the door. "Crap. They're here."

Ivan curled his fingers into fists. "Do you have baseball bats?"

It was time he armed himself and fought back.

"Yeah, we've got a couple of bats in the closet." Brooks peered through the window, his back to the wall. He then moved in closer to get a better look, his breath fogging up the pane of glass. "I think someone's sprawled out--"

"--in front of our door?" Brent asked as he approached his twin.

Genesis '09

"Stay away from the window," Tank said as he pulled Brooks away and blocked Brent from getting too close, but he stole a quick glance down at the street. "It might be watching us." He pulled down the window shades then began to move towards the stairs. "I'll sneak down there and check it out."

"Wait," Brent said, moving towards a door in the hallway. "At least--"

"--take one of the bats with you," Brooks said, nodding in agreement with his twin.

"We know you have one hell of a dropkick," Brent continued as he opened the door and pulled out a silver bat, free of any brand names. "But still--"

"--every little bit helps, right?" Brooks said.

Tank looked at the offered baseball bat, then took it. "Yeah. Every little bit helps." It seemed as if he was reluctant to admit this fact. As if he wanted to be free and independent of such devices.

As Ivan was watching the entire scene unfold, something in the back of his head--instinct, perhaps, or just plain common sense--told him to take action. "I am going vith you," he said, taking the second bat he saw in the closet.

"Like hell you are," Tank said. "You're staying here with the twins, and that's final."

Ivan moved towards the rabbit, holding the bat in a two-handed grip, as if it were a sword. His tail was twitching furiously and he fought to keep from nervously playing with his yin/yang pendant. The memory of Cannon attacking Hopper came unbidden. What if something similar were to happen downstairs? Would even Tank be caught off guard? Unlikely, but Ivan did not want to chance it. "*Nyet.* You may need my help. As you say: Every bit helps."

Tank frowned, but Ivan continued to meet the rabbit's stare. The memory of Cannon and Hopper could not be dismissed from his mind's eye. For a moment, Ivan thought Tank was going to be stubborn and continue to refuse his assistance, but then Tank's expression quickly changed into a warm grin. "All right," he said, rubbing Ivan's head, "but you listen to me, okay? I tell you to run, you *run.* Understand?"

Ivan took a moment to readjust his ball cap on his head properly, then nodded quickly. "*Da.* I understand."

"All right, then," Tank said as he opened the door, inspecting the stairs before motioning Ivan to follow. "Let's go. But if I tell you to run..."

"I vill run, *da.*"

The twins watched as Ivan and Tank entered the stairwell. "I have no idea what's going on--" Brooks said with a shake of his head.

"--but I totally, absolutely *love* Ivan's accent!" Brent smiled.

Tank crept down the stairs, resting the baseball bat on his shoulder. Ivan, on the other hand, held his bat with both hands, ready to swing at a moment's notice of danger. The lights were off downstairs; Tank moved past the light switch, leaving the room in darkness. He spoke in hushed whispers. "You take the right side," he said as he crept his way to the door.

"I'll take the left."

Ivan quietly did as he was told, pressing his back against the wall. The cold he felt was not from the weather. It was from fear. Fear, which he struggled against. He couldn't let Tank down now, not when he pleaded to help him with this. He had to be strong for Tank. For himself.

Tank craned his neck as much as he dared, looking through the pane of glass that separated them from the outside and the body. The frown that furrowed his brow was not a good sign. Ivan involuntarily swallowed--his throat felt dry from Tank's expression.

"Fuck, I knew it." Tank nodded his head at the stairwell. "We need to get back upstairs. It's not there any--"

Tank's words were cut off as the window shattered, scattering glass all over the floor. Time seemed to slow down for Ivan as a hand from outside grabbed Tank's neck, followed by its owner, who tried to push his way in. He was a bear, but the change had already taken effect. A ridge of bone started to emerge just above his eyes, and a pair of horns slowly grew from his temples. There was a glow that leaked out from behind his eyes--a sickly emerald green that hurt Ivan's own eyes to look at them.

Tank's eyes rolled up to the back of his skull and his body started to convulse. The baseball bat fell from his limp hand, and were it not for the monster that clutched at his neck, he would have collapsed to the ground. Ivan knew Tank would want him to run.

The monster howled in pain as Ivan swung the bat two-handed on the thing's forearm. The shriek of the monster sounded exactly like that of the Once Cannon, and there was also the satisfying sound of bones snapping. The monster released Tank, and swiped at the open air where Ivan once stood. He circled around the glass as best he could, grabbing Tank's arm and dragging him away from the monster as fast as his strength could allow.

Tank was already starting to recover; the loss of his strength must have been dependent on continued touch. "Th-thanks, Ivan," He looked for the baseball bat, but it was too close to the monster, who was battering down the door. It wouldn't last under such an assault. "We gotta get back upstairs."

Ivan did not need to be told twice. He pulled Tank to his feet, and pushed him toward the stairwell.

Then he heard the shrieks from the kitchen.

They were surrounded.

The only direction was up. Up the stairs. Which would leave them trapped if there were no exits on the second floor. No matter how durable Tank looked, Ivan doubted he could survive a two story drop without injury. And injuries would only slow them down. Then they would be helpless for the monsters which pursued them.

Ivan kept on glancing over his shoulder to see if said monsters were following them up to the twins, but the stairwell was empty save for Tank and himself. But he knew they were lurking down there. He could *feel* their presence; it made the fur on the nape of his neck frizz out.

The twins were waiting for them near the entrance. Both were wide-eyed with worry. "What was that noise?" Brent asked. "It sounded like--"

"--one of those hoodie guys from that video game," Brooks said.

"Nevermind that," Tank said. "Is there a way to get down to the street without going downstairs?"

Ivan shut the door and pressed his back against it. He wasn't sure the door or his weight could hold back the Once Cannon and its companions.

Brooks nodded. "Yeah, there's a--"

"--fire escape you guys can use--"

"--to get out of here."

Ivan felt a headache form due to the eeriness of the twins' finishing off their sentences.

"You two better come with us," Tank was already searching for the fire escape, then opened up a window. "Mustang'll be cramped, but it's better than the alternative."

The twins didn't need any further urging, their hooves rapidly clopping against the carpet as they approached the window. Tank then directed his gaze on Ivan. "When the twins are outside, I want you to haul ass over here." There was a look in Tank's eyes, one even Ivan could read. Fear.

The twins soon clambered outside and were going down the fire escape when Tank gestured for Ivan. "C'mon, move!"

Ivan pushed himself away from the door in a run, crossing the room quickly. Perhaps too quickly. He was already winded when he reached the window. Too much exertion in such a short amount of time. If he survived--*when* he survived--he would jog more to build up his endurance.

A heavy thud shook the door as he stepped onto the fire escape. Ivan was halfway through the window when he looked over at Tank, who started pushing him forward.

Finally outside, Ivan dropped the baseball bat to the ground just as a clawed hand punched through the door, long fingers scrabbling for the doorknob. He knew the hand belonged to the Once Cannon, which made him hurry down the ladder faster than he liked.

When Ivan heard the impact of the door slamming against the wall, followed by the all too familiar shriek, he looked up.

Tank was gone.

"Ivan! Come on!"

Tank was already on the street.

"How...?"

"I jumped. Get down here!"

Ivan had severely underestimated his lapine companion, but such thoughts were interrupted by the Once Cannon's shriek. Looking up, he could see it crawling out of the window. It had not changed since the last time he'd seen it, but it was still monstrously horrific. Bone spurs jutting out along its eye ridges, it's jawbone, and those *teeth*--like something out of a Stephen King novel. Dripping with a viscous green venom, Ivan feared what it might do should the Once Cannon bite him.

A brick sailed through the air, striking the Once Cannon directly on its nose. It shrieked once again, but this time the pain was evident. It sounded like a chorus of angels.

"Jump down, Ivan! If I can make the jump, so can you!"

Ivan hated jumping from tall heights, but he did as told without hesitation. The thought of Tank *not* being correct did not even try to cross his mind. Tank had proven himself time after time this night, and Ivan felt that any doubt would be an insult to Tank.

Sure enough, Ivan landed on the ground without any difficulty, but Tank still grabbed him by the arm, pulling him up to his feet. "Let's go!" Tank said, pushing Ivan forward.

The car was a classic Mustang, the kind Ivan saw in his roommate Eric's magazines. A Cherry-red, it was in pristine condition. The twins were already in the backseat, and Tank got into the driver's side.

Ivan paused, looking back to see if they were being pursued. The area was devoid of anyone, monstrous or otherwise.

The Mustang's engine growled into life, and Ivan got into the car as if it were urging him to do so. Tank didn't wait for him to buckle his seat belt--he barely gave him time to close the door as the car surged backwards, the tires squealing as Tank hit the brakes hard, sliding the rest of the way towards the street. He hit the gas, and Ivan silently thanked whatever forces might have been watching over him as the Mustang roared forward, taking a sharp turn right. There was no traffic this late in the evening, but Ivan wondered if Tank would have cared.

Brooks glanced behind them, their home quickly lost to sight. "What was--"

"--that thing?" Brent asked, lifting up his sunglasses to peer behind them as well.

Even though they were fleeing for their lives, Ivan had to ask. "Vhy do you vear sunglasses in middle of night?"

Brooks laughed. "Most people ask--"

"-why we finish each other's sentences," Brent said with a grin as he studied Ivan. Brooks did the same, which unnerved Ivan.

"We can see people's auras," Brent said.

Brooks nodded. "The more innocent they are--"

"--the brighter it is for us."

"You're like looking at the sun--"

"--when it's setting."

Ivan looked to Tank for confirmation, who gave him a shrug.

"Tank doesn't believe--"

"--we read auras," Brent said, shaking his head as if Tank had picked his nose in public.

Ivan wasn't sure he believed them either. Him, innocent? Naive, maybe...

...but *innocent*?

"Now we want--"

"--to know what's after you guys," Brent said, casting another glance behind them, as if expecting to be suddenly pursued. Nothing, not even a car, was following them. But Ivan was aware of the nervous tension still hung in the air.

"He's being chased by reanimated transmorphed corpses," Tank said.

Brooks and Brent looked at Ivan with wide-eyes. There wasn't any fear in them--there was awe. This did not make Ivan feel any less relieved.

"Really?" Brent asked. "You're being chased--"

"--by reanimated *transmorphed* corpses?" Brooks said, looking at Ivan with renewed respect.

Ivan nodded, not knowing what a transmorph meant.

"His roomie's pet is the one who got transmorphed the most, according to Ivan," Tank said. "When I saw it knock him down in the gym's parking lot, it was as big as you or Brent."

"Holy crap," Brent said as Brooks whistled low. "That kind of power--"

"--doesn't usually advertise itself." Brooks said. Now there was fear in their eyes. Ivan found he liked that even less. What did it mean when they were only *now* afraid?

"Ivan's got something their master wants. That's why we need to go find Jolly."

"Who is this Jolly?" Ivan asked, tired of constantly feeling ignorant in this supernatural subject.

"Panda. Knows a lot about the supernatural, and he might know who your bad guy is." He glanced in the rear view mirror at the twins. "So where is he hiding this time?"

"He's at--"

"--the old Silver Dollar Club," Brent said.

Brooks held up the baseball bat Ivan had dropped from the fire escape, and he was glad the twins had taken it with them. "We're going to need something better--"

"--than an aluminum bat," Brent said with a slight nod. "Maybe something classic--"

"--like hickory."

"Are you two...vhat is word?" Ivan paused for a moment to consider what to ask. No one tried to help him. "Are you two psychic?"

"Only with each other," Brent said.

"And only if we really try." Brooks added.

"It'd be weird--"

"--if I could read--"

"--my brother's mind--"

"--without trying," Brooks said.

"But you two are completing sentences vithout trying," Ivan said, trying his best to keep up with the twins method of speech.

"That's totally on--"

"--a subconscious level," Brent said, patting his brother's thigh. "You should see us--"

"--when we play poker," Brooks said, smiling at his brother before leaning and nuzzling his cheek.

Tank sighed. "Before you two freak out Ivan with hot twincest action," he said, "might I remind you he's not used to this kind of weirdness?"

Both twins frowned simultaneously, like one was the reflection of the other. A theory that Ivan was slowly beginning to accept as truth.

"We would never--"

"--have sex with each other, Tank," Brooks said, flicking a finger against Tank's ear. "You know why--"

"--we're always touching each other."

"We *have* to," Brooks said, the twins looking back at Ivan. "When we're apart--"

"--for too long--"

"--it makes us feel empty."

"Well," Tank said, "try to keep the kinky twin brother touching to a minimum?"

"We'll try," the twins said in stereo.

Ivan shifted in his seat, clutching his thick, fluffy tail to his chest. So much was happening so fast. He felt as if he'd journeyed to another world, and that his world--his average, *normal* world--was lost forever.

"We're sorry--"

"--if we made you feel uncomfortable, Ivan," Brooks said, leaning forward. "We forget that--"

"--most people aren't comfortable with PDA."

Ivan briefly forgot his discomfort over the twins touching each other. "Vhat is PDA?" Their apology also eased his nervousness. He'd almost expected them to mock his naivety.

Brooks tilted his head, as if Ivan had spoken in his native tongue. "Public displays--"

"--of affection," Brent said. "You've never--"

"--heard of that?"

Ivan shook his head, but before he could explain himself, Tank spoke up. "Let's also not forget that Ivan's being pursued by a grand total of no less than three monsters created by a necromancer," he said as he took the exit to I-80 East. Back to Sparks. Towards the Once Hopper. "So maybe, just *maybe,* it's not you two being all touchy-feely with one another that's bothering Ivan so much."

"It is true. I thought monsters vere only in movies and comic books," Ivan said, burying his nose in his tail's fur. "It is...unsettling. No, it is *terrifying* to know that such things exist in vorld."

Brooks and Brent both placed their hands on either side of Ivan's shoulders. "But there's a lot of good--"

"--in this world too," Brent said. "Like Tank."

Were it not for Tank, Ivan would not be in the Mustang, going to meet with this Jolly, the panda who would surely find a solution to his dilemma. Ivan's only response was to nod in agreement because while he had just met Tank, the twins had seemingly known him for far longer. He felt a pang of...jealousy? He had no idea why he felt it. He just did.

"Once you get past their eccentricities, the twins are good pals too," Tank said, grinning. "Even if they can't keep up with their phone bill."

Brent stuck his tongue out at Tank. "You know why--"

"--we don't keep up with our phone bill. The Order of Pythagoras can trace--"

"--your soul pathways with them."

The twins were less apprehensive now, as if being on the run from monsters was commonplace. Maybe it was. "Order of vhat?" Ivan asked, looking to the twins and to Tank. He thought he knew who Pythagoras was, but what did they mean by soul pathways?

Tank rolled his eyes. "The Order is a myth. A total myth. But what we're running from tonight is totally real." He glanced in the rear view mirror, and frowned. "Is everyone buckled up?"

When Ivan and the twins said they were Tank nodded, but his frown deepened into a grimace.

"Good, because I think we're being followed."

Ivan and the twins looked behind them. A pair of headlights grew as a car approached. Ivan felt his pulse pound against his throat, his fur frizzing out. He forced himself to look at Tank. "Vhat do ve do?"

"We don't panic. Calm down. Smooth out your fur." Tank reached over to rub down Ivan's shoulder. "They try and take you, they'll have to fight me."

Brooks placed his hand over Tank's, followed by Brent's hand over his twin's. "He'll have to--"

"--fight us, too," Brent said.

"You've got allies, Ivan. And when we reach Jolly, you'll have a lot more than just that. You'll have answers."

Ivan topped off the pile of hands on his shoulder with his own. "But... vhat if they have no answers?"

Tank glanced in the rear view mirror. The car behind them drew increasingly nearer. "Then we'll go to the source. I'll go to the source. I'll beat the answers out of the bastard who killed your pop and is harassing you."

Brent leaned forward. "It killed--"

"--your father?" Brooks asked.

"*Da.*" He squeezed his eyes shut. Tank's determination touched him deep within his heart, which no longer beat in fear. The emotion was replaced with another: adoration. "My mama, she told me of this before it came to take vhat belonged to it."

"Some kind of egg," Tank said. He was about to say more, but then the car behind them sped up. Ivan tensed, ready for the collision.

The car moved into the other lane, and quickly passed them.

Tank released the breath he'd been holding. "False alarm," he said, followed by a brief chuckle. "I thought I was going to have to do some crazy daredevil driving again."

Brooks nickered in relief. "I doubt our insurance--"

"--would pay for acts of Tank," Brent said as he slumped back against the back seat, leaning up against his brother.

Tank drove the car to the Pyramid Drive exit. "Here we are," he said. Ahead, the old Silver Dollar casino loomed, illuminated only by the full moon overhead. The doors and windows were boarded up, and there was no traffic in the area. Weeds poked out from the cracks in the pavement. It felt like a forbidden place to Ivan.

"Are you certain he vill help?" Ivan felt like he was in a museum, it was so quiet.

Tank again placed a hand on Ivan's shoulder. "He'll try his best. Trust me."

Ivan had expected Tank to call him out on his repeated questioning. Even Hopper would occasionally look exasperated when Ivan was uncertain about something. But Tank? Tank was patient. Strong in body, soul, and heart. A true friend.

They pulled into a parking spot across the street from the darkened casino, and it was then Ivan leaned forward to kiss Tank on the cheek. "Thank you," Ivan murmured into Tank's ear before he got out of the car.

Tank slowly rubbed his cheek. "Thank me when we've beaten the bad guys," he said with a smile.

Brooks and Brent huddled up against each other. "They make--"

"--such a cute couple," Brooks said with a slight nod.

Ivan pretended not to hear the twins. While he did like Tank, was it because of his actions? Tank saved him more than once tonight. Was this some sort of hero worship? If this night had never happened, would he be as attracted to him?

He tried to focus on the now. Dwelling on what might be a case of gratitude for Tank saving his life could wait. The casino across the street might as well be miles away with the ever-present threat of a sudden attack. "How do ve get inside?"

Tank watched the twins exit the car, then asked "How do we get in, guys?"

"Jolly told us--"

"--to do the Mario Knock," Brooks said.

Ivan blinked in confusion. "Vhat is..?"

Tank rapped his knuckles on the hood of the car. *Tat!* Pause. *Tat!* Another pause, then: *Tat!* "It's important to pause between each *tat*," he said as he took the baseball bat from Brent, "because Jolly, bless his Nintendo-loving heart, might not let you in."

"Vhy call it a Mario Knock?"

Ivan never heard the answer, because he heard a distant screech. "Did you hear that?"

Tank nodded, as did the twins. "We got to hurry." He then urged the twins to start running to the boarded up casino, then grabbed Ivan by the wrist as he ran as well.

A car quickly came into view, the headlights momentarily blinding Ivan as it picked up speed. He had no doubt who was driving it: a once living pug, now transformed into a creature from the darkest of imaginations. He found himself moving faster, now pulling Tank along.

"Dammit, how do they keep on finding us?" Tank asked.

Ivan didn't respond. He didn't look behind him. To see the car as it barreled towards them would paralyze him with fear. Then it would be over, his crumpled body would be delivered to the Once Hopper, and--

Tank pulled him to the side as the car roared past them. It crashed into a row of short metal posts along the side of the curb. "Get to the back of the casino!" he shouted to the twins, then led Ivan around the corner. "Thank Christ those monsters are careless drivers."

"It will soon be after us." Ivan was already feeling his breath burn inside his chest. So much exertion in one night. He was not giving himself enough time to recover. Fatigue was building up in his limbs.

"We'll be inside by then." Tank rounded the corner. The twins were already there. "Knock on the door!" he called out to them.

Brooks knocked on the wood panel three times.

Nothing.

Tank glanced around the corner, then said "You're doing it too fast!" There was fear in his voice. "Don't. Forget. The. *Pause!*"

Brooks pounded on the wall, pausing between each blow. That time the panel between the two groups slid open. The twins ducked inside, followed by Ivan, then Tank.

The panel slid shut. They were safe.

For now.

"Looks like you're in it deep," said a feline as he entered some numbers on a keypad located on the sliding panel. "If it weren't for the cameras, I was about to leave your collective butts out there."

"You're all heart, Scowl," Tank said, giving him the finger.

Scowl looked up at him, a sneer forming on his muzzle. He was a mountain lion, a couple of feet shorter than Tank, which put him squarely at average height. He was constantly shifting his stance, as if expecting something.

When the panel shook from a blow on the outside, he didn't even flinch. Neither did Tank. The twins and Ivan did, and he felt the embarrassed heat fill up his cheeks. He wondered if Brooks and Brent were just as ashamed for showing fear.

"Seems your playmate wants in," Scowl said, jerking a thumb over his shoulder. "Want me to let them in?"

"Tempting, but I think we deserve a rest," Tank said as he placed his hands on the small of his back and stretched. "But since you're here I guess there's none of that, huh?"

Scowl flashed a fanged smile, but there was no warmth to it. "Believe you me, Angus, if this were a social call I'd love nothing more than to toss your oversized ass back outside, but what's trying to get in ain't making it a normal occasion."

Tank's chest puffed out, pecs stretching the fabric of his top as he tensed up. "You couldn't budge me on your best day."

"Want to try me, boy?" Scowl said as he stepped forward.

Ivan found himself suddenly between them, hands held out to block them from moving closer together. "Please, sir, ve are in terrible danger from monsters outside."

Scowl's eyes locked onto Ivan's, and Ivan ignored his instincts to look away. "English ain't your first language, is it?"

Ivan found that question puzzling, but he shook his head. "*Nyet.*"

"You sure you meant monsters? There's more than one?"

Ivan felt his fur bristle under the insinuation. "*Da.*" He lowered his arms to face Scowl. Even though he was taller, Ivan felt like he was at a disadvantage here. Scowl radiated danger. If he was not intimidated by the larger Tank, Ivan was certainly not going to be a threat to him. "There are at least three."

Scowl looked over Ivan's shoulder to squint at Tank. "He's not exaggerating?"

"Nope."

"So what are they?"

Ivan felt the warmth of Tank's hand on his shoulder. It was a welcome heat, and he almost immediately relaxed. "Our best guess is they're reanimated transmorphs," Tank said while he started rubbing Ivan's shoulders firmly.

Scowl turned his attention to the twins. "And the twincest boys are here...why?"

"Because we inadvertently brought them into danger, and they were our only map to you guys."

Ivan saw the twins huddled closer together as Scowl watched them. They were afraid. Of Scowl?

Something the twins and Ivan had in common, then.

"We need to talk to Jolly," Tank said.

Scowl smiled, a gesture which did nothing to ease Ivan's discontent. There was no warmth to that smile. "Sorry to disappoint you, but he's gone out."

"You're lying."

"Usually when it comes to you, I got no problems misleading you, but for once I'm telling you the truth." Scowl looked over at the twins. "Go on, twincest. Tell him."

"He's not lying, Tank--"

"--but he's not telling the complete truth," Brent said.

Scowl's smile vanished immediately, making both twins wince. "Guess you caught me," he said as he faced Tank.

"Where is he?"

"He's sleeping, and I'm not gonna wake him."

Ivan wondered what history Tank had with Scowl to warrant such abuse. He could not imagine Tank doing anything to hurt anyone, but something had happened between these two. "Those things must be destroyed."

"Then do it yourself. Jolly isn't available."

"Vhy let us in if you vere not going to help?"

"You should know, being a feline like me. I like to toy with my prey." He tilted his head towards Tank. "And anything that disappoints this overgrown carrot raider makes me happy."

"I'm sorry, Ivan," Tank said as he started to lead him towards the door. Ivan saw the withering glare directed at Scowl, who merely smiled that cold smile. "Can the twins stay here, at least?"

"No."

The pleading look on Tank's face made Ivan's heart sink. "Come on, Scowl. They've done nothing to you. It's *me* you hate."

Ivan suddenly broke away from Tank, pushed past Scowl and ran through the open door, ignoring the command to stop. After he slammed the door shut, which would barely buy him a second's reprieve, he saw he was inside a darkened hall, but saw a light at the opposite end. He ran down the hall, and pushed himself to move faster as the door opened behind him.

"*Get back here, you damned pus*--" Scowl's words were cut off, followed by a heavy thump, but Ivan was already out of the hall and into room full of empty cubicles.

The source of the illumination came from a lamp at one of the cubicles, and a lion raised his head. Upon seeing Ivan, he quickly stood up. "Who are you?"

"Are you Jolly?" He looked behind him, expecting Scowl to show up and deliver his wrath upon his person.

"It's rude to answer a question with a question, sir. I'll repeat myself: Who are you?"

Genesis '10

"My name is Ivan," he said quickly, fearing Scowl's arrival, "and I am friend of Tank. I need to speak to Jolly."

"And we need to speak to him quick, Robey," Tank said, emerging from the hallway.

Ivan's fur bristled for a second until realized who was at the door. Then he flung his arms around Tank's waist. "Where is Scowl?"

"He got drop kicked. The twins are looking after him." When Tank saw the look of shock on Ivan's face, he grinned. "My ex deserved it."

"This little feud between you and Scowl's gotten out of hand," Robey said as he stepped closer to the two. His mane covered the left side of his face, but the eye that was visible was a bright blue. And angry.

"I totally agree, Robey, but he was aiming his pistol at Ivan here."

Ivan's jaw dropped open as he snapped his head up at Tank, who cupped his hands on either side of Ivan's head.

"It's true, Ivan. Scowl takes his job as security for Robey and Jolly way seriously, but there was no way in hell I was gonna let my ex-boyfriend shoot you."

"Okay, for that I'm sorry," Robey said, rubbing his cheek, then burying his face against his palm. "I warned him about the guns except in extreme emergencies." His eyes wandered over Ivan's form. "And while you're bigger than him, Ivan, I don't think you constitute as a big enough threat for the use of a firearm."

Ivan nodded. "I am sorry for being so much--"

"Hush, Ivan," Tank said, patting him on the head. "Scowl just sees red whenever I'm around. It's something him and me have to work on, but right now we've got to work on your problem."

"So why do you need to see Jolly?" Robey asked, moving to one of the cubicles and wheeling out two office chairs, pushing them towards the duo.

"Ivan's got a necrotic transmorph on his trail," Tank said as he sat down. Ivan did the same.

"Really, now? What'd you do to get one of those, Ivan?"

"Actually, it is three," Ivan confessed, huddling up as close to Tank as he could. These moments of spontaneous bravery were tiring. How long had he been up? Since six in the morning? And how long ago was that? He was weary, but he knew sleep would not be granted anytime soon.

"Three? Damn. I guess I should wake Jolly up." Robey rose from his seat, but a voice from the opposite side of the room made him pause.

"I'm up, Robey. What's this about three necrotic transmorphs?"

Jolly ducked as he entered the room, and he still had to enter sideways. He was literally a giant panda. Much taller than Tank, but where Tank was all muscle, Jolly had a belly. But where most bellies jiggled, his didn't. He could probably take a punch far more effectively than Tank could. His muzzle split open into a wide yawn, then scratched around his prodigious girth. "Who's your friend, Tank?"

"This is Ivan," Tank said. "Ivan, that's Jolly."

"Pleased to meet you, Ivan. Forgive me if I don't shake hands yet, because I'm seriously wiped out. Had a infestation at the last safe house yesterday." He moved towards the trio, dwarfing Robey as he stood behind the lion. "So, about these transmorphs. Tell me what you know."

Ivan did not ask what kind of infestation. The more he learned of the world outside his viewpoint, the more it disturbed him.

Tank leaned his shoulder against Ivan's, bringing him back into focus. "Come on, Ivan. You can tell these guys. They'll believe you just like me and the twins did."

Ivan took a breath, held it, then slowly exhaled through pursed lips. "All right." He then began his tale, starting with the moment Cannon died, to the strange pursuit of the bee, followed by Cannon's return, the appearance of the egg in his room, the attack on his roommate, followed up by his possession and culminating with Ivan's flight.

Jolly and Robey listened without interruption, their eyes never wavering from Ivan. When he was finished, Jolly stood up, scratching his chin. "Sounds like a necromancer," he said.

"Hate those bastards," Robey growled, his tail lashing fiercely behind him. "But what's the deal with the egg?"

"Don't know," Jolly said, moving to the computer. "Some kind of magical talisman?"

"That's obvious," Tank said. "But why doesn't the necromancer just take it? Why make Ivan his go-to boy?"

Ivan then suddenly remembered something he forgot to mention to Tank and the others. "He was very disappointed that I did not know who he vas," he said. "Something about the true history of the old country."

"A necromancer of the old country being Russia?" Jolly asked.

"*Da.*"

Robey sat in front of the computer desk, and typed on the keyboard. "Well, let's see what Google can find for us." A moment later he squinted at the computer screen. "Three hundred and thirteen thousand entries for 'Legendary Russian Necromancers'.

"I'll make some coffee," Jolly said with a grimace, then looked at Ivan and Tank. "Why don't you two try and rest? You both look like hell."

Tank pulled out his cell phone. "Sure, but I need to check my voice-mail. Got a call while I was running for my life, and I'd like to at least return the phone call before I start fighting for my life again."

The room was on the second floor, and it was remarkably clean. Jolly and the others had been prepared to use this abandoned casino for some time. Although Ivan was not sure he could sleep, he found himself drifting away the moment his head touched the pillow. His sleep was dreamless, and when he woke up, Tank was sitting in the corner, watching him.

"Sleep well?" Tank asked, a frown creasing his forehead.

"As vell as expected," Ivan said, sitting up with a yawn. The inside of his muzzle felt like it had a coat of velvet.

"You were out for about an hour, Latté."

"It did not..." His voice trailed off.

Ivan never told Tank his nickname.

Tank held up his cell phone. "The call I got was from Hopper trying to set us up on a date. Yeah, he's my cousin. I didn't know you roomed with him. Stupid provider didn't send me the call until after we got chased." He scowled at the cellular device. "I'd change providers, but I think it saved my life."

Before Ivan could ask Tank explained. "If I'd gotten the call, I would've known who you were. Hopper was very thorough in describing you, and there aren't many snow leopards built like you." A grin appeared on his muzzle. It seemed very forced. "Hell, I don't think there are any snow leopards in Nevada. The heat alone in summer would fry them."

Ivan drew his knees towards his chest, his arms curled around his legs. "Hopper told me you vere bouncer at bar."

Tank lowered his head to stare at the bed. "I got the gym job last week. Hadn't spoken to Hopper in two. Still, if I'd known...I would have charged right on over to your apartment to fight that guy. And I would have lost." He met Ivan's eyes, and held it. "I would have been killed, and you would be in big trouble."

"You still do not know me. I still do not understand vhy you go through all this."

Tank had his chair turned backwards, and his arms rested along the backrest. He rested his chin on those crossed arms, letting loose a sigh. "Maybe you'll understand, and pay it forward. You know, what you supposedly owe me."

"Are you angry vith me?" It never occurred to him that Hopper and Tank were related, but now that he knew their relation, he *could* see a resemblance. The identical color of fur. The solidity of their build. How had he not noticed this even before this supernatural insanity intruded upon his life?

Tank got up from his chair to sit on the bed next to Ivan. "No, no. I was pissed off when I put two and two together, but it wasn't directed towards you." He cupped Ivan's chin, fingers stroking the fur. "I'm angry at the son of a bitch that's taken control of my favorite cousin's body. If I can't save him..." He paused for a moment, his eyes starting to water. "If there's no way to bring him back..."

Ivan looped an arm around Tank's waist, brushing his fingers along the lapine's chin like how Tank had done not seconds before. "Your friend Jolly vill help us."

Tank wiped his eyes with the back of his hand as he pulled away from Ivan's embrace. "Yeah. You're right. Sorry for losing it there."

If that was losing it, what had Ivan done before they had met the twins? A total mental breakdown? "You are stronger than I can ever be."

"You keep on underestimating yourself. That'd be so cute if we weren't being chased by monsters." Tank said as he got up to move towards the door and opened it.

Suddenly Tank stumbled back as Scowl stood in the doorway, rubbing his fist.

"We're even for your little kick to the head, Tank," Scowl said, then vanished into the hallway.

Ivan rushed over to Tank. "Are you all right?"

Tank looked at his finger, which was spotted with blood. "Yeah. Good thing Scowl hits like a girl."

"He moved so fast, I did not see him leap up to hit you," Ivan said, looking for something to stop Tank's nosebleed.

"Yeah, he's been studying some crazy martial arts for years. Tai Quan whatever, I dunno." Tank braced himself against the wall, placing a finger against his nose. "Damned grudge carrying ass," he said as he took the towel from Ivan. "It's bad enough I have to watch out for monsters, but now I have to watch out for ex-boyfriends?"

Ivan sat on the bed, looking out into the hallway, afraid that Scowl was still out there, and waiting to further assault Tank. Without Tank, what would he do? He could not fight the monsters by himself.

"I'll be all right, dude. Just gotta catch my breath is all." Tank stood up, examining the towel. "Damn, that's a lot of blood," he murmured before suddenly leaning back against the wall again.

Ivan was immediately at Tank's side, bracing him should he fall. "You do not look vell," he said, guiding him to the bed. "You should rest."

"I'm fine," Tank said, though he remained on the bed. "Dammit, if Scowl messed with my chakras, I'm gonna curb-stomp him."

Ivan didn't know what chakras or curb-stomps meant, and he doubted he wanted to know. "Stay here. I vill go downstairs and get you vater."

Tank had a dreamy look in his eyes, as if he had just woken up. "Your accent is so cute, you know?"

Ivan frowned. Tank was losing focus. Was it a concussion? He didn't know how to check for one. Would it be safe to leave Tank like this? Would they hear him if he shouted? "You need to come vith me. I am vorried for you." He ducked under Tank's arm and tried to help him up.

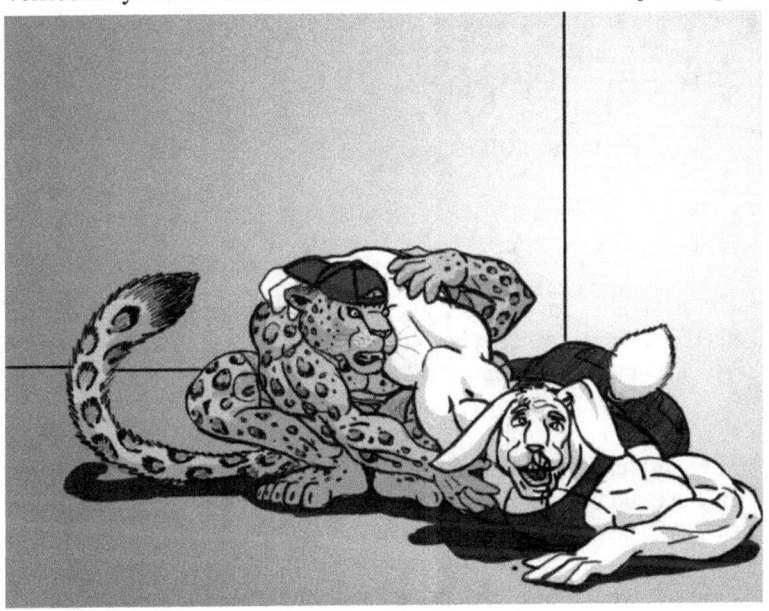

Tank was dead weight, and Ivan could not budge him. "Aw, I'll beeee all right. Bee. You were chased by a bee yesterday, remember?" Tank was staring straight ahead, his eyes were unfocused.

"I remember. Do you remember your cousin is in danger? Ve have to help him." He hated to use Hopper as motivation, but what else could he do? He wasn't strong enough to carry Tank.

"Ye...yeah. Hopper." Tank squinted, and Ivan saw the determination return in those eyes. "I...I can't lay down. I gotta help."

Ivan managed to get Tank up on his feet, and while the progress was slow going--Tank almost stumbled halfway down the hall--they made it to the first floor. Scowl was nowhere to be seen, but Robey, Jolly, and the twins were clustered around the computer.

"I think it's the old crone. The self-proclaimed Mother of Russia," Robey said.

"But there's no mention of an egg," Jolly said. "I think you might be wrong about this." He looked up and saw Ivan and Tank enter. "What happened to Tank?" he asked as he helped move Tank to a chair.

"I think Scowl hurt Tank's chakras."

"Jesus Christ at a Lada Gaga concert. When will these two grow up?"

"Vill he be all right?" Ivan asked, taking up his tail in his hands and carefully stroking the fur.

Jolly pulled back Tank's eyelid, studying the pupil. The silence bothered Ivan, and he felt relief when Jolly said "Yeah, I think Scowl just desynched the crown chakra. He'll need to rest for a day."

A day without Tank's assistance was not good. He didn't know this new group well enough to trust them, and while Jolly was quite a bit larger than Tank, did he have the experience to fight monsters? Tank seemed to have confidence in their capability, but... "Are you certain?"

Jolly gave Ivan a look he could not identify. Was the panda annoyed? Patient? "He'll be fine. Don't worry. We're not going to let those monsters have you, but even if they did catch you...I think the worst they would do to you would be to take you back to their master."

"Which I'm not sure is the old crone."

"Who is the old crone?" Ivan was lost. Adrift without Tank by his side.

"You think it's safe to say her name, Robey?"

Robey nodded, brushing back his mane, though it still covered one eye. The keyboard clicked away as he typed. "Yeah. I think they know we're here anyway."

Jolly folded his arms, leaning back against the wall as he kept his eyes on Tank. "We think your monster is Baba Yaga, a powerful sorceress who also moonlights as a cannibal."

A lump started to form in Ivan's throat. His mouth went dry. "This is bad, yes?"

"I still say it's not her, though." Jolly shrugged as he pushed himself off the wall and lumbered over to Robey. "For one thing, there's nothing linking her to an egg."

"And I have to admit," Robey said, leaning back and running a fingertip along the back of Jolly's hand, "there's nothing linking her to necromancy." He took Jolly's hand with both of his, and kissed the panda's thumb. "And there's no mention of an egg."

"So that means we're back to the start of our search," Jolly said. "Sorry, Ivan."

Ivan continued to brush his tail. They could not help him. They were as lost as he was.

"Can't believe Google failed us," Robey growled as he released Jolly's hand and went back to typing. "Maybe I need to try some new search terms. Maybe use folklore instead of fables."

"Can't hurt," Jolly crouched down to watch the computer screen. "Wait. What's that?"

Ivan's ears perked up.

Robey peered closer at the computer screen. "We could have saved a lot of time if we had, oh, I don't know, used the right search terms."

Jolly stood back up. "Well, Ivan, I think we've found your man. Koschei the Deathless."

"Is he as bad as Baba Yaga?"

"I'll be honest. Scowl's going to get the riot act for fucking with Tank. We could really use him, and I don't think we can afford to wait."

This news did not comfort Ivan.

"So this...this Koschei the Deathless..is very dangerous individual," Ivan said.

"He's a powerful necromancer," Jolly said with a grim nod, "but he also has one particular weakness if what we read is true."

Ivan's ears perked up at the word weakness. While he would have been more comfortable with Tank's help, perhaps all was not lost. "Vhat is his weakness?"

"That egg," said Jolly. He tapped the computer screen with a claw. "He put his soul in a needle hidden inside that egg. As long as his soul is separate from his body, he can't die. This says the egg was hidden inside a duck, which was inside a hare, which was in an iron chest buried under an oak tree on Buyan island in the middle of the ocean. Open the chest, the rabbit runs off. Kill the rabbit, the duck flies away. The point is to keep the egg away from anyone who tries to take it." He arched an eyebrow at Ivan. "Did your father ever go to Buyan?"

"When I vas baby,Poppa once mentioned trip to island, yes, but he vould not say vhy."

Jolly rubbed his chin. "According to this, whoever possesses the egg also possesses Koschei's power. It weakens him, wears him out. He can't get to his magic. Chuck the egg into the air, and Koschei gets chucked in the air along with it. He's helpless. Except..." He shook his head. "Somehow I don't think the part where he's weakened is true if he can create monsters, but the first part..." Jolly's voice trailed off, and his eyes gained a far off look to them. He was soon lost to thought.

"Vhat are you thinking?" Ivan did not like being left out of these thoughts. It was his life at stake, and perhaps the life of Hopper's as well. "Please, tell me vhat you are thinking."

Jolly blinked, leaving Robey to chuckle. "Don't mind Jolly," he said, "he's got a mind that has a dozen thoughts. Each of them goes at least a mile a second."

Jolly ruffled Robey's mane. "I've only got half a dozen thoughts. I'm nowhere near as smart as you. Or as pretty."

"It's the conditioner I use. Great for the mane."

"Lucky you." Jolly then turned to face Ivan. "Anyway. I think there's some merit to the part about being in possession of the egg puts Koschei in the owner's power. If he's so powerful, why didn't he just take the egg? You said he wanted you to give it to him, right?"

Ivan nodded. "So you think egg cannot be taken from him? That egg is still in my room?"

Jolly pointed a finger at Ivan, winking at him. "I would bet you a dinner at a casino buffet if your life weren't in danger." He looked back at the screen. "Anyway, supposedly the only way to kill him is to destroy the egg. Or maybe the needle. I'm not sure which is the right solution, so we should just destroy both."

"Do you have plan?" Ivan asked, feeling hope blossom inside his chest again.

"I just might, Ivan. I just might."

"Do we have any holly in our garden?" Robey asked. "It works against malevolent spirits, and it worked against that one sorcerer."

Ivan blinked in surprise. Even though he now knew magic existed, it still caught him off-guard to hear of the secrets the world kept. Of magic. Of monsters.

"I think we're out, but maybe some of that black cohosh would work."

"Vhat is black cohosh?"

Jolly suddenly gave Ivan a wan smile. "Oops. Sorry. Forgot you were a civilian."

"Oh, this should be good," Robey said with a smirk. He leaned back in his chair, leaving part of his mane to continue to cover his left eye. "Go on, Jolly. What's black cohosh good for, hm? If you don't tell him, I will.

Feline unity, and all that."

Jolly shot Robey a look. One that even Ivan could translate. *We'll talk later*, it said. "Black cohosh gives courage to the meek if carried. No offense."

Ivan shook his head. "I am not offended. I am surprised I did not give up at the very beginning, vhen I saw roommate's pet turn into monster."

"You're braver than most people when faced with something beyond their comprehension," Jolly said. "You got spirit, too, from what Tank and Robey told me, defying Scowl like that." He looked at Robey. "Speaking of our favorite asshole, where is he?"

"Guarding the door like nothing happened."

Jolly frowned. "I think I'll go have a brief chat with him, see if he knows about our holly and black cohosh stock."

"And maybe toss him around some for messing up Tank?"

Jolly's frown turned into a grin. "He needs to get over what happened between him and Tank. It was almost a year ago."

"Please hit him once for me," Ivan said. When both Robey and Jolly gave him surprised looks, he added "He hurt my friend."

"Don't worry, Ivan, I'll have a nice chat with Scowl." Jolly then lumbered towards the hallway. "As a matter of fact, I'll go do that now. Don't worry about the noise."

Ivan then remembered the twins. He did not see them leave, and felt a momentary rush of concern for the two. Where had they gone? "Vhere are Brooks and Brent?"

"They're napping. They were exhausted after having to make sure Scowl wasn't going to suffer any ill effects from being drop kicked, though I almost hoped his personality would get flip flopped like last time." Robey then shook his head. "But we didn't get so lucky."

Outside of the room Ivan heard muffled shouting, followed by a heavy thud that shook the wall. "Oof," Robey muttered. "I didn't think Jolly would be that rough with him."

A few minutes later, Scowl entered the room with an expression Ivan would not have expected to see--worry.

Genesis '10

Robey stood up quickly. "Where's Jolly?"

Scowl rubbed the back of his head, unable to make eye contact with Robey at first. "I fucked up, Robey. He's out cold."

Robey took two quick steps, then stopped, teeth bared in a growl, hands clenched into tight fists. "I could have sworn you just said Jolly was out cold."

Scowl did not reply. He started to look away from Robey, who snarled "God *dammit*, don't you look away from me, Scowl! What the hell did you do? No, don't bother answering." Robey then pushed past Scowl and entered the hallway. Presumably to Jolly.

Ivan gave Scowl a furtive glance, not wanting to make full eye contact. He didn't think Scowl would strike him, but the feline carried a gun. Angry people did dangerous things at times, and Scowl always seemed angry.

Jolly was on the floor, unconscious. Robey had forced one eye open and was shining a penlight on it. "God damn that Scowl. His crown chakra is scrambled even worse than Tank's," he said, a single ear turned towards Ivan when the snow leopard entered.

"I'm sorry, Robey," Scowl said, causing Ivan to spin around and stumble back. This caused a ghost of a sneer to appear on Scowl's muzzle. "Jolly looked pissed, and I was still pissed, and when he tried to lunge at me, I--"

"I said don't bother answering, you evil son of a bitch," Robey said, kneeling down and getting his thighs under Jolly's head, stroking the giant panda's cheeks. "You just did this because you didn't want us helping Ivan, huh?"

"Vhat?" Ivan glared at Scowl, who actually flinched. "I have never met you until now."

"It's not like that. Robey's just upset."

"You're damned right I'm upset, but it's true. You think Ivan is Tank's new boyfriend, and you just hate that fact."

Scowl's eyes narrowed into slits while he bared his fangs in a snarl. "Bullshit."

It made sense to Ivan, though. Tank's affection towards Ivan--rubbing his shoulders, both of them going up into the bedroom. Scowl was jealous. "No. Robey is right. You think I am Tank's lover."

"I don't give a damn if you are or not."

"No, you do. And I pity you."

Scowl's eyes widened in surprise. Shock. And most of all, anger. "Pity me?"

"You still love Tank, but you cannot let him go." Even though his heart was racing when Scowl narrowed his eyes and his muzzle was deepening true to his nickname, he continued to speak. "You vant him, but he does not vant you anymore. And it hurts you because he understands you better than your friends."

"Bullshi--"

"Shut up, Scowl--"

"--you're a bitter, miserable thing," Brooks said, the twins frowning behind Scowl. They were holding hands, as if getting strength from each other.

Scowl looked at the twins, then at Ivan, then at Robey. He finally settled his gaze on Ivan. "I hate you. I don't even know you, but I hate you. Because Tank looks at you like he used to look at me before things went south on us."

Ivan wanted to run, but there was nowhere to run. So he fought back. "I forgive you."

Scowl's muzzle twisted into a hateful sneer as his hands balled up into fists. "You *forgive* me? For what, knocking out your wannabe boyfriend?"

Ivan wanted to hit Scowl for that. Yes, he was attracted to Tank, but the rabbit could do so much better than a cowardly snow leopard like himself. "*Nyet.* I forgive you for being unable to see past your anger and hate."

Scowl flinched as if slapped. "I don't want your forgiveness." But there was something in his eyes. A hint that maybe he was lying. Maybe he craved forgiveness. Maybe he was trapped in the spiral of those destructive emotions.

"And I do not care." It was hard to stay brave under the growing fury of Scowl's temper. Would he be struck down like Tank and Jolly, or would Scowl be the first to look away? "You can escape this misery journey you are in, but I vill not be one to help you. I must help myself." He broke eye contact with Scowl to look at Robey. Somehow it did not seem like a loss. "May I use your computer to read up on this Koschei myself?"

"Yeah. I'm going to stay here." Before Ivan turned away, Robey looked up at him. "I'm sorry, Ivan. Scowl's not always like this, but..."

Ivan nodded. He understood. Exes held great influence on those who could not let go. That much he had learned this night. As he walked past Scowl, the cougar growled quietly "You think you won this fight, don't you?"

Ivan paused, then shook his head. "*Nyet,*" he whispered. "But you have gained nothing as vell."

Scowl would, most likely, never escape the downward spiral of his hate and anger. Not even with friends like Robey and Jolly. He was lost. Like Ivan could have been had Tank not helped him.

He moved down the hallway, his heart racing. Did he just stand up to someone who knocked out two men who were even bigger than him? He would not have done that before the events that led him here. Tank's bravery in the face of danger obviously inspired him. Or perhaps he was not as much of a coward as he believed.

Anyone possessing the egg has Koschei in their power.

So confusing. His entire life had changed in the space of one evening. And as he seated himself in front of the computer, he was going to do something he'd never done before.

Break the egg, or break the needle, and Koschei will die.

He was going to disobey his mother. He was not going to run anymore.

In some stories, the egg must be broken against Koschei's forehead. It was the only way to be sure.

All he needed to do was destroy both items. The only question remained: Could he get close enough to the Once Hopper--to Koschei-- and complete his task?

He would try. It was all he could do now. He was not going to run anymore.

Koschei was going to pay.

Ivan heard someone approaching. He didn't recognize the scent. Was it Robey? Or was it...

"You're going to need help getting there," Scowl said, leaning up against the door frame.

"I vill ask Robey or the twins," Ivan said as he turned back to read the information on the computer monitor. The response made Scowl chuckle.

"Robey's not going anywhere. Not after what I did to Jolly. It really was an accident, you know."

"I know." Ivan was not going to make eye contact with Scowl again. It made him feel drained, having to look into those dark eyes. He needed all of his strength. He also needed to sleep for a week. Sleep was not going to be high on the priority list, however.

"And twincest can't drive in combat situations. They're pretty useless in a fight, unlike me. I'm your best chance to get in, get the bad guy, and then come back to make sure your squeeze'll be all right."

This time Ivan did lock eyes with Scowl, who grinned as if winning a fight. "Tank is not my squeeze." He wasn't sure if he knew what a squeeze

DEATHLESS

meant. "He is my friend."

Scowl moved into the room, his grin now transformed into that hateful smirk. "This is probably true, but sooner or later you two'll be bennies."

"Vhat are bennies?"

"Friends with benefits. You know, pals who knock boots with each other." When Ivan continued to look confused, Scowl sighed heavily as he rolled his eyes. "Sex, you ignorant cat. You two are going to have sex."

Ivan felt his cheeks burn with anger; his fur poofed out as he squinted at Scowl. "I am tempted to make hurtful mistake."

Scowl looked confused. "Hurtful mistake?"

"I am vanting to try and hit you. It vould be hurtful mistake, since you are fighter. I am not fighter. I vould lose."

Scowl grinned toothily. Like all his other grins, this one was unpleasant. Ivan wondered if the mountain lion had any kind of grin that *were* pleasant. "Tell you what. I'll give you a free shot." He patted his chest. "Go on. Hit me. I owe you that much."

"No," Ivan said with a shake of his head, "I vill not resort to your level."

Scowl frowned, folding his arms. "And my level is exactly...what?"

"Violence is second nature to you. You respond vith violence. You act first, and regret later."

"Can't argue with that. It's something I've been dealing with all my life." He shook his head. "But you don't care about my past and I don't care to explain myself." He jerked a thumb over his shoulder. At the hallway. "When you're ready, let me know. I'll drive."

Now it was Ivan's turn to frown. "I did not say I vould accept your help."

Scowl shrugged. "I didn't ask if you were going to accept it."

Ivan looked away from Scowl. "I do not like you."

"Likewise. So let me know when you're ready to go."

Ivan watched Scowl leave the room. Annoyance welled up inside him. Why did people like Scowl get away with so much, and then gain forgiveness so easily? If he did not need help in reaching his apartment where the Once Hopper--where Koschei the Deathless--lay in wait, he would refuse any help the mountain lion offered.

Sighing, he got up and made his way to the hotel room where Tank was sleeping. He crouched at the side of the bed, placing a paw on the rabbit's hip. "I vill be back, Tank," Ivan murmured into his long ear, which twitched slightly. "If I do not..." The words trailed off. He could not finish his speech. He leaned over to kiss the rabbit's cheek, and made his way back to where Robey tended to Jolly.

Ivan could hear them talking in quiet voices. Too quiet for him to make out what they were saying, but it sounded like they were planning. When he entered the room, Scowl and Robey looked over at him. "I am ready to go," he said.

"We got stuff for you," Scowl said, holding up a small soot-colored drawstring pouch the size of a quarter. "Tie this around your wrist. It's got some plants that will hopefully ward of whatever voodoo this Deathless guy uses."

Ivan took it from the mountain lion, the apprehension blossoming in his chest. "'Hopefully'? You are not certain?"

"Magic's not an exact science. If you believe in it hard enough, it should work."

Ivan had never even heard of Koschei the Deathless. It was hard to believe in something just introduced to him. "I vill try," he said as he tied the drawstring around his wrist. "How vill this place be protected vhen you leave?" he asked Scowl.

Scowl arched an eyebrow. "Robey'll protect the place."

"Robey is attending to Jolly," Ivan pointed out.

"Chances of any real danger coming here is unlikely."

"Is that vhat you thought before I arrived?"

Scowl grew quiet, then looked over his shoulder at Robey. "He's got a point."

"I'll be fine, Ivan. The twins will help me carry Jolly to a room."

Ivan studied Jolly. Bigger than Tank, who did not have the solid belly Jolly had. "Jolly is big panda. Are you certain you vould not be better off with Scowl here?"

"You need Scowl more than we do." The doubtful expression on Robey's face told a different story. How well would the twins be in a fight? How well would Robey fight?

Ivan had a thought. It was a dangerous one, but if what he believed to be true...if the legend was correct... "I think I have plan."

As he told them of what the plan entailed, their expressions went from one of doubt to one of grim acceptance.

"This plan of yours might work," Scowl said. "I'm impressed, pussycat."

Ivan ignored the insult beneath the compliment.

"But what if you're wrong?" Robey asked.

Ivan did not have an answer for that.

"If this plan doesn't work--" Scowl began, but was cut off by Ivan. A feat of bravery (and rudeness) which surprised the snow leopard.

"If this plan does not vork, you all vill be safe. It is me they vant, not you. They vere only after Tank because he came to my aid."

"He's good at that," Scowl said, a dark look crossing his face. "He'll come to the rescue until he realizes you're not wanting to *be* rescued." He then smirked up at Ivan. "But I'm sure you'll hear his side of the story if you survive this."

If. Not when. Scowl most likely did not care if Ivan survived. Yet he did offer to assist him. Perhaps he was not a complete bastard.

"Now let's get your fluffy ass out of here and hope that the monsters leave us alone, or at least alone enough to get to the car." He gave Ivan a quick once-over. "Can you handle a gun?" When Ivan shook his head, the mountain lion shook his head as well. "Typical. Your Mommy was probably afraid you'd shoot your little fluffy toes off."

Ivan kept his muzzle shut, glancing over at Robey, who shrugged. *Sorry,* he mouthed.

Scowl tilted his head at the door. "Let's jet," he said, pulling out his pistol. Ivan didn't recognize the make, but it looked like the kind of gun a bad guy would have in those countless action films his roommates would watch. Very solid looking, and perhaps could even slow down the Once Cannon.

Ivan felt a pang of longing for those simpler times. Would he ever get to see those movies again with Eric and Hopper? He hoped so.

The door slid open, quiet as a whisper, and Scowl went outside first. The night was at its darkest--Ivan had lost all sense of time. For all he knew it was almost dawn, which would be a welcome sight for his eyes and soul. "All clear," Scowl whispered.

"Good luck," Robey said as he stroked Jolly's forehead.

"Thank you," Ivan said as he followed Scowl.

The door slid shut just as quietly as it had opened. The night air was still. Nothing moved. There was not even a car on the interstate. This most of all made Ivan apprehensive. Even at this late time, there should be some traffic over there. "Alright," Scowl said, his voice still in that hushed whisper, "where's the car?"

"It is in front of casino. Across street."

Scowl held the gun in a two-handed stance, barrel pointed up. "Okay, follow me."

They kept close to the wall as they crept towards the front, and once at the corner, Scowl motioned for Ivan to stop. The mountain lion looked around, his eyes searching for enemies. He then beckoned for Ivan to follow, and they both ran across the street.

Before them was the twins' Mustang in the parking lot where they had left it, untouched.

An obvious trap.

Ivan began to doubt his plan now.

The headlights of the Mustang flared to life, cutting through the darkness and blinding Ivan. It didn't take long for his vision to recover, so he was able to see the car doors open slowly. The once pug slid out of the driver's side; he was unchanged, but Ivan caught his scent, which had changed. It was an intense odor, like he'd been dead and rotted for weeks. On the other side slid out the Once Cannon. Its scent was unmistakable, but it was even taller than before--it seemed to unfold once out of the car. It flexed its long fingers, the talons glinting in the light. It looked down on him with a quiet hiss.

Ivan stood his ground, and did something which even surprised him: he bared his teeth at the Once Cannon in a snarl. It blinked once, then twice. As if its brain could not comprehend the snow leopard being brave. Perhaps it expected Ivan to cower.

He was happy to confuse it.

"Fuck me sideways," Scowl said. "We're surroun--*hurk*!"

Ivan turned around and saw Scowl, his body rigid as the once bear had the cougar by the throat. Like the Once Cannon he was almost unrecognizable as an ursine. Scales of bone surrounded his brow, forearms, chest and shoulders. Scowl was not struggling, and Ivan recalled what the bear's touch did to Tank. Scowl's eyes then rolled back in their sockets, and he went limp. When the once bear released him he crumpled like a rag doll.

Ivan backed away from the bear, pug, and the iguana. He did not wish for Scowl to be hurt, even if the cougar deserved it. Perhaps running would save him. It was him they wanted. Scowl would be left alone. Maybe.

No. While the old habits of running were dangerously instinctive, he would *not* run. He had a plan and he was going to stay the course.

He stopped his retreat.

He raised his hands in front of him.

The monsters paused, hissing their confusion at him.

"I give up," Ivan said.

The Once Cannon drew itself up to its full height. Did it understand Ivan's words? How intelligent *was* the Once Cannon? How powerful was Koschei the Deathless and his magic?

"I surrender." This time he spoke in his native tongue. Perhaps they did not understand English. Perhaps they did not understand anything but their master's commands.

Koschei needed him alive. Ivan prayed this also meant unharmed. But what if Koschei could kill him and subsequently resurrect him? He could then command Ivan to give him the egg, and--

The bear lunged at him, grabbing him by the throat. Immediately his neck went numb, and the numbness spread through his body like fire followed by darkness.

* * *

When Ivan opened his eyes, it took him a moment to register where he was--inside his apartment. Back where he started. And Koschei stood over him, smirking. Triumphant.

"Now, kitten," Koschei said, "you vill give me the egg."

Koschei frowned, which looked odd, since he was inhabiting Hopper's body. The Once Cannon was curled up along its master's side, the Once Pug and Once Bear close by. <Go fetch me my egg, kitten,> he said, his voice distant and cold. <If I must motivate you, perhaps your hyena friend will be useful.>

Eric! Was he home? Ivan whipped around towards his roommate's door, which brought out a dark chuckle from Koschei. It disturbed Ivan to hear such an evil sound from Hopper's voice, even if he knew it was not really his friend.

<Yes, kitten, your friend arrived not long after you left. Do not worry, I merely put a spell on him to sleep. It is good to not waste potential tools, would you not agree?>

Ivan disliked the thought of his friends as tools, but to argue the point would prove unwise. His instincts screamed at him to fight or flee. Fighting was out of the question, as was flight. He slowly rose to his feet, eyes narrowed and focused at his bedroom door. His body shook in a mixture of growing fear and rising anger.

<You are wise to keep your temper and fear from forcing you to do foolish actions,> Koschei said. <Continue to keep your emotions at bay, and you will live to see the dawn.>

Ivan slowly moved towards his bedroom. He would take the egg, give it to Koschei...and what after that? Live to see the dawn, then die at the hands of a legend? While Koschei promised he would leave Ivan alone after the delivery, how did he know the necromancer would keep such a promise?

His hands and feet felt like lead weights, his body tense from fighting every instinct he'd ever possessed. His heart was racing, his fear was screaming at him to run, and his anger wanted to be released in the form of several blows to Hopper's possessed body, particularly his head.

To do any of that would mean his plan would fail. Ivan could not allow himself to ruin his plan.

Inside the bedroom everything was left as it was prior to the nightmare that had started earlier in the evening. The egg with its perfectly white shell sat next to the phone. It seemed more like a pearl than some object laid by a hen. It glistened in the fluorescent light.

How he wanted to smash it, but he doubted it would break. If the legend were true, it could only be broken if smashed against its creator.

He would soon put it to the test.

His thoughts were abruptly derailed by the electronic ringing of the phone, though it was so faint he almost thought it was his neighbor's. Glancing over his shoulder to see if anyone was approaching, he grabbed the receiver. Who would be calling?

"Hello?"

The voice which replied spoken in perfect Russian, though the accent was...odd. <You will listen to what I have to say.>

<Who...is this?>

<I dislike questions, but I will answer yours this once. My name is Baba Yaga.>

<Baba Yaga...> Ivan glanced over his shoulder again. Certainly Koschei would grow impatient, and begin to wonder what was taking the snow leopard so long to retrieve the egg. The voice on the other line must have sensed his thoughts, and agreed.

<You must stop your foolish talking, kitten,> Baba Yaga said, her voice sounding as if it came from the depths of a cavern. The tone chilled Ivan more than the coldest winter in Russia. <You must use the egg to protect yourself.> Before Ivan could ask how, she continued. <Take the egg and command Koschei with your mind and your voice. Do not allow him any room for misinterpretation. You will say exactly what I am about to tell you.>

Ivan listened, or at least tried to as his thoughts were distracted by the impending approach. Certainly Koschei would send his monsters into his room. Then all would be lost. He would not be able to avenge his father's death.

<Repeat what I told you, kitten,> Baba Yaga commanded, her voice now clearer, as if she were approaching, and not Koschei's minions.

Ivan did as was told. Why was Koschei being so patient? Why was he allowing Ivan time to plot?

<You worry so much, kitten,> Baba Yaga chuckled, a horrific sound like metal scraping upon metal. It forced Ivan to grit his teeth. <I realize you know nothing of Russia's true history...> She almost sounded... disappointed? Sad? <...but certainly after all that has been said and done tonight you would also understand nothing is absolute. Not even time.>

Ivan glanced at his clock. It was digital, so he could not check to see if the voice on the other end of the phone was boasting, or... <You...are that powerful?>

<I dislike questions.>

<I didn't mean to ask-->

<I will allow your ignorance of my rules to go unpunished,> Baba Yaga sighed, a sound like that of a breeze drifting through a crypt. It was ancient. Ivan could feel the weight of many years in that sigh. <If only because of your father's loyalty.>

<My father?> Ivan pressed the phone closer to his muzzle, lowering his voice to a whisper. <What did he-->

<I dislike questions, kitten. Your ignorance will only go unpunished for so long, and there is no time for explanations. Do as I told you. Use Koschei's egg. We shall speak again.>

The line went dead. Ivan stared at the phone and listened to the dial tone for a moment before putting it back on its cradle. Had that conversation really happened? Did the Grandmother of Russia truly contact him and gave him the information to put his plan into motion?

Most importantly, could her information be trusted?

Ivan took the egg from its place on his bureau. It felt so fragile. Yet it did not give when he indulged in the temptation to squeeze the shell. He would not be able to break it.

He left his bedroom.

Towards Koschei.

One of them would die.

<I was almost thinking you would need my pets to help you out of your bedroom, kitten,> Koschei said, a hateful sneer on his muzzle. <But I see you have found your way out.> His eyes fell upon the egg held in Ivan's paws. <And you have brought me my egg. Good.>

Koschei did not mention the phone ringing. Baba Yaga had prevented the necromancer from hearing their conversation. Ivan had hope; his plan stood a chance of succeeding.

The Once Cannon hissed at Ivan, as if sensing something. Perhaps it detected the hope Ivan carried in his heart. He refused to give it up. Around the necromancer the others shifted, as if nervous.

<My pet does not like you, kitten,> Koschei said as he rubbed the side of the Once Cannon's horned head. <You gave her quite a chase, and forced me to make other servants to grant her aid. They, too, do not like you.> Koschei looked directly into Ivan's eyes, and the snow leopard forced himself to not flinch from the hateful gaze. <I do not like you either.>

<Will my friend be free of you once you leave his body?> Ivan asked, covering the egg with his free paw.

Koschei frowned. He also seemed surprised. Perhaps he did not expect Ivan to be so brave. He was too used to the snow leopard who ran. The snow leopard who did not fight back. <Yes. His soul still resides within this body. He will awaken with no memory of what happened, and I will rid him of the memories of this night.> His grin was too wide, and exposed too many teeth. Ivan did flinch this time, prompting Koschei to chuckle. <Better. You show proper respect.> He held out his paws, slowly clenching and unclenching his fingers. <Now give me my egg. I would enjoy going home.>

Ivan swallowed the lump that was forming in his throat, and took a deep breath to slow down his racing heartbeat. If it pounded against his chest any harder, it might burst out from the confines of his ribcage. <*Da,* but first would you kindly send your servants away? Perhaps to the Bullseye store?>

Koschei nodded. <Of course. No need to cause you undue problems, yes?> With a flick of his wrist, the Once Pug and Once Bear trundled away, outside the apartment.

<Once they are at the store, you will kindly release them from your control, yes?>

Koschei smiled warmly, tilting his head down and spreading his hands. <But of course, kitten.>

<*Purity of spirit,*> Ivan recalled Baba Yaga's words, <*is necessary to keep Koschei the Deathless under control while you possess the egg. It is also a matter of basic politeness. We of the Old Country appreciate manners.*>

<Thank you, sir.>

<You are welcome, kitten. It is no problem at all. Now if you would give me my egg, I will be on my way.>

Ivan took another deep breath, closing his eyes shut as he rehearsed the next request to himself. He was close now. He was so very close.

<I will give you your egg, sir,> Ivan said slowly, making sure every syllable was clear and succinct. There was no room for error. The first mistake would quite possibly be his last. <But first, could you restore Cannon to her original state before she became your pet?>

Koschei looked down at the Once Cannon, who seemed...puzzled. As if it could not understand why Ivan still held the egg. Koschei himself seemed to look at it as if seeing its transformed state for the first time. <Of course,> he said amicably. <How rude of me to keep it in such a state. I will not be able to take it with me. My apologies.>

With a single gesture of his hand and words that Ivan felt more than heard--words which Ivan hoped he would never, *ever* hear again--the Once Cannon stiffened, then slowly curled up into a fetal position. The disturbing sounds of bones cracking, reknitting, reshaping themselves filled Ivan's ears as it slowly shrank down, the protrusions that riddled its body slowly withdrawing. Before long, she was a small, dead iguana. As if she had never become a terror during the evening.

Ivan swallowed hard, his mind trying desperately to cling to his former viewpoint of reality, and failing. He saw the transformation before his very eyes. It really happened. Even after all the events of the night, seeing something that he thought was impossible a week--even a *day*--ago left him in a frightened awe. <Th-thank you, sir.>

<You are welcome, kitten. I do not mean to repeat myself, but may I please. Have. My. Egg?>

Ivan fought down the panic in his stomach. Koschei would soon realize the subtle control, so he had to act fast. <Yes, of course. If you would just hold out your hands...> he said as he approached Koschei, the egg held out in front of him.

Koschei held his hands out, cupped together.

<And if you would kindly not move while I give you the egg, it would be greatly appreciated.>

A dark look crossed Koschei's face. <What is happening?>

Ivan would later think of at least a half dozen phrases he could have uttered, most of them taken from the dozens of action films his roomies made him watch. But instead Ivan slapped the egg against Koschei's forehead, the white shell fragmenting into dozens of pieces before vanishing into tiny puffs of vapor. A tiny pin was stuck on Koschei's brow, and before Ivan could do anything it broke in two. Then it drifted away in twin puffs of black smoke.

Koschei's eyes grew wide, then he sank to his knees, then collapsed on his side against the floor. Ivan was afraid to see if he was still alive. Worse, Ivan was afraid he might still be Koschei and not Hopper.

Then the rabbit's eyes flew open.

"Hopper?" Ivan said, unable to keep the hope from his voice.

"Ivan?" What'm I doing on the floor?"

***

Ivan sat on the back of his roommate Eric's cherry red truck. It was a delightfully cool afternoon in April, so Ivan did not feel too out of place going shirtless. A can of diet soda dangled from his fingers as he stared off into the distance. He could not see the gym thanks to the Bullseye store, but he knew who would be working there.

After the events of that fateful night, he had checked up on Tank. Hopper had no recollection of anything, he didn't even have a scar from the iguana bite, so he was clueless as to why Ivan wanted to visit an abandoned casino at the crack of dawn. Robey and Scowl assured him that Tank was fine.

And then he saw Jolly.

It took them an hour to explain what had happened. That while Ivan had been napping, Baba Yaga contacted them over the Internet, and told them if they did not leave Ivan to face Koschei alone, then she would kill Tank.

Then it took them a half hour to calm Ivan down. He felt betrayed. They misled him, but the only reason he did not storm off was he had lied to them as well.

His plan was to grab the egg and throw it at Koschei in hopes of it striking him on the forehead. The plan he lied about was approaching Koschei and then smashing it against his forehead. Or trying to. Using the egg to temporarily subdue the necromancer had never occurred to him.

So why did Baba Yaga help him? Why did she care if he lived or died? He was afraid to find out, especially after reading up on her mythos. She was sometimes shown as an antagonist, and sometimes as a source of guidance; there were stories where she helps people with their quests, and stories in which she kidnaps children and threatens to eat them.

He learned that seeking out her aid was usually a dangerous idea. Perhaps even fatal.

Ivan also learned why she disliked questions. If the legends were true, and Ivan suspected very strongly they were, she aged one year every time someone asked a question. Dislike was an understatement. She probably *loathed* questions.

So why did she tolerate his questions, even for a short time? What was he to the Grandmother of Russia? Why did she want to help Ivan's desire for revenge?

He finished his diet soda, and walked over to the trash bins. The same bins he ducked between when on the run from the Once (and finally deceased) Cannon.

Hopper had eventually gotten another iguana. This one, he named Koschei.

Ivan hoped it was a coincidence, but he doubted there was any such thing anymore. Robey assured him there were no signs of any possession, so perhaps in some part of Hopper's memory he was aware of what happened, and naming the iguana was how he coped.

Ivan started jogging.

He was good at running away from things.

The cool air ruffled his fur as he ran, his legs pumping at a steady pace. After the events of that night, he found himself wanting to build up his stamina, especially seeing as how Tank's seemed limitless. Ivan occasionally questioned his reasons for aerobic exercise. Did he really want to build up his endurance for health reasons, or was he unconsciously jealous of Tank's prowess?

Ivan remembered how, on the day after things returned to a sense of normalcy, Tank showed up at his apartment, looking as healthy as he did when Ivan first met him. The only thing different about him had been the sheepish look on his face.

"I'm sorry I couldn't stick by you through the end of your adventure, Ivan," he had said.

"There is no need to--"

"No, there is. I made a promise and I couldn't keep it." Tank leaned up against the door frame, shaking his head. "I keep my promises, and I feel like crap that I let Scowl catch me off guard." His eyes met Ivan's. "I was supposed to protect you."

Ivan smiled up at Tank. "You did your best, and I am alive because of you."

Ivan grinned at the memory. Tank was a gentle soul in a behemoth lapine body, and Ivan liked him. They had started working out together, and Tank proved to be a perfectionist, correcting Ivan's workout techniques anytime the snow leopard was less than perfect. He would also lavish Ivan with praise whenever his technique was perfect.

All in all, Ivan's life had improved significantly since the events of that night. His mother was deliriously happy when he called her the next day--after she scolded him for disobeying her. Still, she was grateful that the nightmare was over for Ivan and his family.

And yet...there was the knowledge of how much more there was to life. Most of it sinister and potentially deadly. Magic was real, and there were shadow organizations. It was terrifying to know that such things exist in the world, but like the twins said there was a lot of good in the world.

Like Tank.

Tank, his knight in lapine form. Tank, who saved him from death.

Ivan owed him his life. How could he ever repay such a debt? He knew he did not want to fight the threats Tank and his friends fought, but certainly there was something he could do.

The knowledge of such things that he previously never believed existed could not be erased. Could he fully return to his old life?

<You cannot, kitten.>

The sudden voice in Russian at his side startled him, but he continued his rhythm. It was a young child who jogged with him, dressed for the weather. She grinned up at him.

Ivan did not know who this young child was, and looked around for her parents. <Who-->

The child's grin turned immediately into a harsh frown. <I dislike questions, little kitten.>

A chill blossomed in Ivan's spine, filling up its length. <Baba Yaga.>

<Yes. You learn your lessons well, kitten.>

Ivan almost asked why she was here, but caught himself. <You honor and terrify me with your presence, Grandmother.>

Baba Yaga cackled, which unsettled Ivan as it came from a child's lips. <You *do* learn your lessons well, kitten. Respect *and* honesty? I am impressed.>

<Thank you, Grandmother.> So many questions he wished to ask. Could he dare to ask one? <If I had known you were going to visit, Grandmother, I would have...> What was it again? <...I would have made you your favorite tea. With the blue roses.>

Another cackle. <Clever little kitten. Asking me if I have my tea without asking. It will please you to know I made a special cup before I visited. You may ask your questions carefully.>

Ivan almost stumbled; he slowed his pace. <Then I suppose...why did you help me?>

<Because I owed your family a debt, kitten. Shortly after you were born, your father went to the island of Buyan to retrieve Koschei's egg.> She stared straight ahead, a frown on her muzzle. <He did so under my request.>

This time Ivan did stumble. After he caught his footing he stared at Baba Yaga. She did not meet his eyes.

<Your family has served me well over the years. Your father kept the egg from Koschei, but he made a fatal mistake. He grew careless, and Koschei found him. Before I could intervene, your father died.> Her voice grew soft. <He was mourned by more than just you and your family.>

<I have more questions, Grandmother.>

<Speak your mind, kitten.>

<Why did you keep Tank and his friends from helping me?>

<You cannot always depend on the help of others.>

Ivan arched an eyebrow. <But *you* helped me.>

Baba Yaga smirked, an expression out of place on the child she possessed. <I *advised* you. It was your choice to accept or reject it.>

Ivan wanted to call her out on such a double standard, but he kept silent. Baba Yaga must have sensed his disdain. <It took much of my power to send you Koschei's egg,> she said. <I would expect some measure of gratitude.>

Ivan quickly caught his temper before it flared out of control. Had she not sent the egg to him, Koschei might have very well killed Ivan's mother and brother. <And you have it, Grandmother. Your advice saved me.>

<So it did.>

<I have but one more question.>

<Good. I am quickly running out of tea and patience.>

<What happens now?>

<You may live your life however you want, kitten. Your family will be cared for, and you may continue your studies in the States, though I do hope you will not forget your roots.>

<My body is not there, Grandmother, but my love will always dwell in Russia.>

<I once had a big, fluffy tail like yours, kitten.>

Ivan hesitated. <It must have been beautiful, Grandmother.>

<I had to cut it off because I almost choked. I shall never have snow leopard children again.> She grinned toothily up at him. <Farewell, kitten.>

And then she was gone.

Ivan stared at the empty space where Baba Yaga had been. The information given to him, plus the unsubtle reminder of what he was speaking to left him feeling cold. He was close to his destination, so he decided to continue his jog.

He crossed the street and arrived at the gym. Tank's truck was parked in the side lot. *Early as usual,* Ivan thought as he entered the building. While he signed in, he saw Tank emerge from the locker room.

"Hey," Tank said, grinning. He was shirtless, like Ivan, but looked better than the snow leopard. Less fur did wonders for definition.

"Hello, Tank."

"No, no," Tank said, shaking his head. "Say it in Russian. I want to see if I got the pronunciation right."

Ivan rolled his eyes in mock irritation. "*Zdravstvuj,* Tank."

Tank's muzzle scrunched up in a slight frown. "I thought it was *Zdravstvujtye.*"

"That is usually for more than one person."

Tank's expression brightened. "Ah. Gotcha." He had been learning Russian a week after the events of that night. 'To better understand you', was his reasoning.

A few minutes later, Ivan was changed into his workout shorts, and the two did their routine for the day. It was upper body, which was something Ivan had a slight edge in over Tank, oddly enough. When they were done, they retreated to the locker room, and Tank took a shower. "Ivan?" he called out from the stall.

"Vhat?"

"You give any thought about Scowl's offer to train you in his martial arts style?"

Ivan had, indeed, given it plenty of thought, but he still was not sure if he ever wanted to learn it. How Scowl used it frightened him, and he would never want to have that kind of skill, even if he would use it responsibly. "I am still uncertain if I vant to learn from him."

"Don't blame you," Tank said, emerging from the shower with a towel wrapped around his waist. "Him and me...we're trying to talk, but he still acts like it's my fault we broke up. I don't like it."

Ivan knew what direction it was. He could still see the love in Scowl's eyes for Tank. He also saw the embers of love in Tank's eyes, but they were dying.

Love was a hard flame to extinguish, but it could die out if not given fuel to burn.

Tank turned away from Ivan, letting the towel fall. The snow leopard took this time to stare. Tank was a handsome specimen. Noble. Part of him was happy to know that his love for Scowl was not as strong as it used to be, and the other part felt guilty for that happiness.

"Tank? Vould you like to go see movie tonight?"

Tank looked at Ivan as he put on his pants, his hands paused while bucking his belt. "Sure. I'd love to."

Life was filled with terrifying things. Things that lurked outside of the awareness of most people. But life was also filled with good things.

Ivan needed to try to hold onto at least one of them.

About the Author

Graveyard Greg is a writer of webcomics like Dungeons & Denizens (http://www.dungeond.com) and Gaming Guardians (http://www.gamingguardians.com). He also writes fiction (in case you didn't realize it from this story), and is a terrible devourer of sushi.

You can find him lurking on Twitter at http://twitter.com/graveyardgreg

www.ingramcontent.com/pod-product-compliance
Lightning Source LLC
Chambersburg PA
CBHW071328130626
46556CB00004B/1799

* 9 781935 599623 *